Published in Nashville, Tennessee, by Tommy Nelson™, a division of Thomas Nelson, Inc.

Scripture quotations are from the *International Children's Bible®, New Century Version®:* Copyright © 1986, 1988, 1999 by Tommy Nelson™, a division of Thomas Nelson, Inc.

Creative director and series consultant: Dandi Daley Mackall
Computer programming consultant: Lucinda C. Thurman

Library of Congress Cataloging-in-Publication Data

Holl, Kristi.
      Tangled web / written by Kristi Holl ; created by Terry Brown.
         p. cm. – (TodaysGirls.com ; 3)
      Summary: Alex is unhappy living with her mother's parents in Indiana while her mother and alcoholic father remain in Texas, and her life becomes more complicated when she uses her computer to act on her suspicions about her grandparents' new neighbor, who Alex is certain is a criminal.
      ISBN 0-8499-7562-X
      [1. Prejudices—Fiction. 2. Grandparents—Fiction. 3. Family problems—Fiction. 4. Christian life—Fiction.] I. Brown, Terry, 1961- II. Title. III. Series.
PZ7.H7079Tao 2000
[Fic]—dc21

                                                                                    00-024414
                                                                                            CIP

Printed in the United States of America
00 01 02 03 04 05 QPV 0 9 8 7 6 5 4 3 2 1

TANGLED WEB

WRITTEN BY

Kristi Holl

CREATED BY

Terry K. Brown

Tommy
NELSON

Thomas Nelson, Inc.
Nashville

Web Words

2 to/too

4 for

ACK! disgusted

A/S/L age/sex/location

B4 before

BBL be back later

BBS be back soon

BF boyfriend

BRB be right back

CU see you

Cuz because

CYAL8R see you later

Dunno don't know

Enuf enough

FYI for your information

G2G or **GTG** I've got to go

GF girlfriend

GR8 great

H&K hug and kiss

IC I see

IN2 into

IRL in real life

JLY Jesus loves you

JK just kidding

JMO just my opinion

K okay

Kewl cool

KOTC kiss on the cheek

LOL laugh out loud

LTNC long time no see

LY love you

L8R later

NBD no big deal

NU new/knew

NW no way

OIC oh, I see

QT cutie

RO rock on

ROFL rolling on floor laughing

RU are you

SOL sooner or later

Splain explain

SWAK sealed with a kiss

SYS see you soon

Thanx (or) **thx** thanks

TNT till next time

TTFN ta ta for now

TTYL talk to you later

U you

U NO you know

UD you'd (you would)

UR your/you're/you are

WB welcome back

WBS write back soon

WTG way to go

Y why

(Note: Remember that capitalization may vary.)

chapter.1

Alex Diaz yanked her best friend Morgan into her bedroom, then slammed the door. "Gotta keep the heat in," she said, shivering dramatically as she turned up the room heater. "I will *never* adjust to living in the frozen North."

Morgan refastened her hair with a silver clip. "It's only Indiana, not Alaska."

"Could fool me. This room is colder than any igloo. You know what January's like back in Texas? No frostbite. No ice on windshields. No blue lips."

"But no canceled school for snow days either!"

"Okay. That's *one* good thing about it." Alex wiggled the mouse by the computer, and her screen came to life. "Doesn't matter anyway. I'll be back home before you can say Rattlesnake Roundup." Alex had already lived half her ninth-grade year with her grandparents, but her dad had finally found another job before Christmas. "My folks'll send for me any time now."

Alex hiked up her jeans and pulled her corduroy jacket close around her. At five-two, her jeans dragged the ground and the sleeves of her jacket hung over her fingers. Her long curls were impossible to tame, and she didn't try. Grandpa stared at her wild hair like she was an alien from another planet.

"Come on, come on," Alex muttered as she logged on to the Internet. This computer had been the only thing keeping her from going stark-raving mad since being exiled to Siberia, but it was *so slow*.

"You're lucky you have this computer to yourself." Morgan dragged a vanity bench over beside Alex's chair. "Maya and I had to share one for six years!"

"Grandma uses it, too, for stuff like this."

Alex shoved aside a Neighborhood Watch notice scribbled in her grandmother's spidery handwriting. Grandma McGee, a retired teacher, had volunteered at the middle school for years. When their library was upgraded, Grandma had bought a used computer cheap.

Alex's password was verified, followed by squeaks, honks, and beeps. "Chill while I check my e-mail, then we'll get in the chat room."

"There's probably nobody there anyway." Sighing, Morgan laid the back of her hand to her forehead. "Only us lowly fresh-men sit home on Saturday night."

Alex frowned as she read her only e-mail, an ad from a sporting goods e-catalog. She'd only heard from her mom once that week, a short note written at work. Usually her mom e-mailed from work three or four times a week. Alex's stomach churned. Was her dad drinking again? Was her mom missing work, like during his last drinking binge when her dad started throwing things?

Two nights earlier Alex had tried to call home, but the phone was disconnected again. It happened every time they got behind on their phone bill. Alex chewed a hangnail. Something was rotten in Texas . . .

Morgan huddled over the heater. Blinking, Alex leaned over and turned the heat up. "Don't worry. It'll feel like Miami Beach by bedtime."

Turning back to the computer, Alex clicked on TodaysGirls.com in her bookmark file. The screen flickered as the girls' private Web site loaded.

Long before Alex had moved to town the previous August, Morgan and her friends had been meeting online in other chat rooms. To avoid the weirdos that lurked everywhere, they'd usually created private rooms. Then Amber, a junior, and Morgan's sister, Maya, had designed their own Web site.

At last the site appeared. "Welcome to TodaysGirls.com!" pulsated in silver and purple. Jamie's cartoon in the Artist's Corner showed a huge mouse sitting at a computer, a tiny man gripped in its paw.

At the top of the pink screen, Amber's Thought for the Day announced a new weekly theme about not judging others.

"Amber should be a preacher," Alex muttered, "one of those TV ladies with perfect hair and acrylic nails." Alex curled under her own bitten nails, embarrassed by how stubby her brown hands looked.

"Amber's cool once you get to know her," Morgan said. "You guys just got off to a bad start."

Alex shrugged. Blonde and beautiful, Miss Perfect Amber was everything Alex wasn't: popular, preppy, and too nicey-nice to be believed. It had to be fake. Fuming, she waited while Morgan read the Thought for the Day aloud.

"'Don't judge other people, and you will not be judged. . . . Why do you notice the little piece of dust that is in your brother's eye, but you don't notice the big piece of wood that is in your own eye?' Matthew 7:1–3."

Whatever that means, Alex thought, clicking on the chat icon and typing in her password. Just then a curled Post-It note dropped from the side of her screen.

"What's that?"

"Just an old reminder. When y'all invited me to join the chat, I couldn't keep y'all straight." She smoothed out the scribbled note:

Bren = *chicChick*
Amber = *faithful1*
Jamie = *rembrandt*

Maya = *nycbutterfly*
Morgan = *jellybean*

Beside Alex's own name, she'd crossed out *newkid*, replacing it with *TX2step*. Rolling her eyes, she remembered how she'd had to explain what a Texas two-step *was*. Alex tossed the old note in the garbage.

The names faithful1, nycbutterfly, and rembrandt were listed in a column on the right-hand side of the screen. TX2step was highlighted in red.

nycbutterfly: ICU, TX2. LTNC. Where U B????????? : (
TX2step: With Morgan. we rented a movie
nycbutterfly: Don't mean 2nite. U've been MIA 4 3 days.
 Splain.

Alex frowned. "MIA? Missing in action?"

"She means missing practice. Coach was really bugged that you skipped."

Alex hunched her shoulders, feeling attacked. "If I want to skip swim practice, it's none of their business."

"No, but it's hard practicing our relay without you."

Like I need this hassle, Alex thought. Alex swam on the relay team with Morgan, Maya, and Amber. She'd held the freestyle title for two years in Texas. She hardly needed the practice. Besides, she'd been working on a plan this week to get back home soon. She had to find out what was wrong there. So why go to practice? Still, to keep her escape a secret, she couldn't afford to make them suspicious.

> TX2step: no sweat, Maya. B there Monday.
> faithful1: we miss U, TX. I filled in 4 U, but we stunk. We
>   need U!
> nycbutterfly: RO!
> TX2step: Morgan says get off my back.

Morgan poked Alex on the arm, then pushed her hands aside and typed "I did not!" and hit *Send.*

> faithful1: peace, GFs, we've got other things 2 discuss.
>   Alex & Morgan, we need UR help on something else.
> rembrandt: we need UR talent & beautiful faces!
> nycbutterfly: NW! we need UR elbow grease 2 earn big $$$
> faithful1: TX, U can dance the 2 step. kick up UR heels
>   4 a good cause?

"What's she talking about?" Alex asked.

"Beats me."

> TX2step: no talent here. wuzzup?
> rembrandt: we're performing 4 old people @ a shelter.
>   I paint scenery. Amber 2 sing. We need U. Wanna B
>   in a skit?

nycbutterfly: Morgan and Alex can sing a duet.
TX2step: O no we can't! I howl like a hound dog.
nycbutterfly: old people r deaf anyway. won't matter. if
    U won't perform, then U 2 can give $$$ 2 it.
TX2step: Sorry. I don't have a job like Jamie.

And I wouldn't work at the Gnosh Pit like Jamie if I was starving, Alex thought. It was just another sorry excuse for a restaurant, even if Morgan's parents did own it.

Indiana was full of disgusting food. Alex hadn't had a decent enchilada since being shipped north. Or chili or hash or hush puppies either. For Pete's sake, they didn't even know that "Coke" meant *any* kind of carbonated drink . . . they all drank *pop.* Salsa came in jars, and when you asked for guacamole, waitresses looked dumber than dirt.

Morgan cracked her knuckles, then her knee joints. "Dad wants me to work at the Gnosh, too."

"I guess you kinda have to, but no way am I sucking up to customers all day. That 'customer is always right' junk is pure garbage."

faithful1: No job? NBD. I have jobs lined up already thru
    the youth leader @ church. Come on, U 2, help us out.

Morgan raised an eyebrow in Alex's direction. Alex shook her head, then chuckled as she typed.

TX2step: I'm fixin 2 run. Grandma's calling. good luck
with your little talent show. G2G SYS :)

"Whew! That was close." Alex yawned. "If I wanted something pointless to do, I'd do my homework."

"Me, too." Morgan rolled up her sleeves and moved away from the heater to flop down on Alex's bed. "How come you're skipping practice? The big meet's Tuesday, you know."

Alex slumped over the keyboard, wishing Morgan would drop it. She could hardly explain that she was getting ready to run away. "I'll be there Monday morning."

Opening her bookmark file, she scanned her list of favorite sites. She found the Internet fascinating—worlds of escape no farther than the click of a mouse.

Turning suddenly, Alex knocked her math book off her desk. Half-finished worksheets fluttered out. "Why learn all this junk anyway? I'll never use it."

"Aren't you going to college?"

"No way, Jose! I'll start a business on the Internet. Then I'll travel all over the world and take my job with me. I'll never be out of work," she said, recalling the painful months each time her dad was laid off.

"I love history. Maybe I'll lead tour groups at famous historic places."

"Ugh! You'd have to dress up. No way am I wearing pantyhose and shaving my legs all the time."

Morgan hooted. "Most of us *do* shave for the swim team," she pointed out.

Alex pulled up one pants leg to reveal dark stubbly hair. "Who invented that stupid rule? Girls in Europe don't shave."

"You're casting heavy shadows there. Maybe you could curl it."

"Suppose if I shaved every day I could swim faster?"

Just then a sharp rap sounded on the bedroom door. "Alexandra?" her grandfather called. "Are you still on the Internet?"

Alex heaved an exasperated sigh. "No, we're off." Her voice dropped to a whisper. "Yesterday he called the Internet an 'instrument of the devil.' Talk about paranoid."

"Don't forget about church tomorrow," he added.

Alex gritted her teeth till her jaw ached. Every time she turned around, they were dragging her to church or a potluck supper. She drew the line at midweek Bible studies. "No wonder my mom ran away when she was sixteen," she whispered.

"Really?" Morgan sat up cross-legged on the bed. "Why?"

Alex immediately regretted her words. "I dunno really. Just all the hassles, I guess." She grabbed her pajamas from under her pillow and headed to the bathroom. There she changed and scrubbed her face with Ivory soap. She knew, from being in the shower room after practice, that her friends used special facial cleansers and moisturizers. The day she could afford special cleansers pigs would fly.

On the other hand, maybe she could invent a low-cost fancy facial cleanser to sell over the Internet. Prickly Pear Cactus Scrub, anyone?

Turning, Alex stubbed her toe on the claw-foot bathtub, then limped down the hall to her bedroom. Her hand was on the doorknob when Grandma stepped out of her own room. Although Alex and her grandmother were both five-foot-two, Grandma outweighed her by several years' worth of homemade cinnamon rolls and fried chicken.

Grandpa's voice barked from their bedroom. "Emily! What did you do with my reading glasses?"

"I never had them."

"I saw you take them. Something about wiping off the smudges."

"I did?" Grandma blinked like an owl waking up. "I'll look for them." She winked at Alex, then padded down the hall.

When Alex opened the bedroom door, she was struck by a blast of hot, stuffy air. The heater was working overtime now. She closed the door for privacy, but crossed to the window and pushed it up two inches, sticking a book in it so it wouldn't fall down.

Morgan was back in the chat room and didn't glance up. "I just wanted to ask Maya something, then I'll get off."

"Don't worry. Grandpa's gone to bed." Alex perched on the bench beside the desk, brought her knees up to her chest, rested her chin there, and read while Morgan chatted.

rembrandt: Did U C Shelly's new haircut? What was she thinking????

nycbutterfly: She looks like her brother now. JK
faithful1: I think she looks kinda cute.

Morgan rolled her eyes. "Amber's too good to be true. Shelly looks like an escapee from Alcatraz."

nycbutterfly: Can U believe the English assignment?
    There's no way I can write a 5 page report using
    poetic devices. ACK!
faithful1: What a drag. My favorite subject these days is
    BIOLOGY!!
rembrandt: I thought U couldn't stand Kistler.
faithful1: Who's talking about Kistler? Have U seen the
    nu student teacher?
nycbutterfly: Ooo, honey, I wouldn't mind if he helped
    me dissect my pig lung.
jellybean: LOL Didn't know U had any. Must B hard
    swimming w/pig lungs!
nycbutterfly: Ugh. Freshman humor. Morgan, Mom says
    4 U 2 come home w/me after church tomorrow. I'm
    going w/Amber.
jellybean: K

Alex rolled her eyes. Must be tough to have your biggest problem be poetic devices, whatever they were.

Ten minutes later Alex left to get a drink of water, and when she returned, Morgan was already in bed. Her black hair, fastened with a band on top of her head, resembled a waterspout.

"Lovely pajamas." Giggling, Morgan leaned up on one elbow. "Where'd you get 'em?"

Alex glanced down at her ruffled flannel pajamas with big romping kittens splattered all over them. "Grandma remembered I love cats. She just forgot I'm not seven anymore."

"Well, it's the thought that counts."

"Yup." Actually, as retarded as they looked, Alex liked the idea that Grandma had noticed she needed pajamas. At home, she slept in sweats, then half the time wore them to school the next day. She kicked aside her flip-flops, then crawled under the covers.

Morgan rolled over on her stomach. "Did you see Sarah talking to Amber's brother at lunch today?"

"The great Ryan Thomas was speaking to a little freshman?"

"Yeah, and now she'll say he likes her 'cause they exchanged hellos."

Alex snorted at that. "To him, we're just Amber's little girly friends."

"Just wait till lunch Monday. Sarah will spend the whole lunch break trotting back and forth to the snack line, trying to run into him again."

"And squealing. I hate when she squeals."

Morgan squealed in imitation, which set them both off. For the next half-hour, they shared the horrors of being the only mature freshmen in a sea of immature children. Finally, Morgan sighed and rolled over toward the wall. "'Night," she said, her voice already drowsy.

"'Night." Alex turned off the bedside lamp.

The room was plunged into blackness. Alex threw off her blanket, irritated that she was now sweating when an hour ago she'd been freezing. Texas was never this irritating. It was warm and predictable. Grass stayed green, food was hot and spicy, and precipitation arrived in one form only: water. In Indiana you never knew if you'd get rain, sleet, snow, hail, or fog.

Without warning, lonely thoughts of Texas washed over her. Her home might be a thin-walled trailer in a run-down mobile home park, but it was still home. She'd give anything to be there right now. Her mom needed her—she knew it in her gut. *Hang on, Mom,* she thought, *just a little longer.*

Lying on her side, Alex noticed a light come on next door. Then a back door slammed, and Alex gritted her teeth. Couldn't those new people show some common decency and be quiet? A car door then squeaked open and slammed shut. The back door slammed again. *Good grief!* Alex fumed.

"Matthew! Come back here! You can't drive alone!" yelled a deep voice.

Morgan rolled over, her voice groggy. "What's going on?"

"I dunno." Alex slipped out of bed and peered out her second-story window at the neighbors' house below.

The boy in the junky car was Matthew. He sat next to Alex

in computer class, when he bothered to show up. He and his dad had moved into the vacant rental just a few weeks ago. Grandma had taken "Hutch," the older man, under her wing, but Alex had distrusted him from the first.

"Come back inside," Hutch called.

"Think you can make me?" Matthew yelled back.

At that, Hutch threw himself off the porch steps and onto the hood of the car. The car engine roared to life and jerked into reverse. Alex gasped in horror as Hutch slid off the car and hit the frozen ground.

chapter.2

Morgan, come here." Alex pressed her forehead against the cold window.

Below, Hutch lay sprawled on the gravel driveway, illuminated by the car's headlights. Matthew had opened his door and cussed loud enough for the whole neighborhood to hear, then cut the engine. Hutch crawled to his feet and brushed the snow off his knees.

"Are you trying to get yourself killed?" Matthew yelled.

"No, trying to prevent that happening to you." Hutch's voice was several decibels lower, but still audible with the window open. "You only have a driver's permit. Anyway, it's too late to go out."

It's a little late to be screaming under someone's bedroom window, too, Alex thought in disgust. She glanced at the digital clock's glowing red numbers: 1:12 A.M.

Morgan peered out the window. "Who's that guy?"

"Matthew something," Alex whispered. "He sits by me in computer—" She was cut off by another outburst from below.

"Look who's talking," Matthew shouted. "You come and go at all hours. You're never here, so why should I be?"

"Now, son, that's not true—"

"It *is* true!" Matthew pushed past his dad and disappeared inside.

Hutch limped over to the car, reached inside, and turned off the headlights. Alex couldn't put her finger on it, but there was something weird about him . . . He gave her the creeps, although her grandparents sure liked him. They'd even invited him to church. Even worse, once Alex had overheard Grandpa telling Hutch all about Alex's dad and his drinking. Like it was any of Hutch's business! Well, Alex had her eyes peeled. Hutch's halo would slip one of these days, and then she'd show Grandpa a thing or two.

Below, Hutch shuffled over to the garbage cans by his house. He bent over the first can, pushing his arm in deep. Then he pulled it out.

"Yuck. What's he doing?" Morgan asked.

"Who knows?" Alex's eyes opened wide. "Wait. I bet I know. I lived in a bad neighborhood once and saw a drug dealer stash dope in his garbage can to hide it. When the police came, they never even looked there."

"You think he's a drug dealer?"

"Or worse. I know he doesn't have a regular job."

"Matthew *did* say he was out all hours of the night."

"Sounds like something illegal to me." Alex hoped so.

Just then Hutch glanced upward, right at Alex's window. Gasping, Morgan jumped back. "It's okay. He can't see us." Alex hid behind the curtain just the same. "Look. He's heading this way!"

Hutch crossed the adjoining driveways and disappeared from sight directly under Alex's window. She smashed her face against the glass, but could no longer see him.

"Is he breaking in? Wake up your grandparents!"

"Wait. Listen. He's right below. He just dropped our trash can lid. He's poking in there, too." She couldn't believe her luck. She was only seconds away from nailing this creep. Alex grabbed Morgan's hand. "Come on. And not a sound."

"I'm not going out there!"

"Then stay here. I'll catch Hutch in the act by myself." Alex snatched her oversize shirt from the floor and flung it on without buttoning it. Fishing under the bed, she pulled out her flip-flops.

"Wait. I'm coming." Morgan grabbed the comforter off the bed and wrapped it around her shoulders, then jammed her feet into untied sneakers.

With one hand on the cold plaster wall, Alex felt her way down the L-shaped hallway, tiptoeing past her grandparents' door. She paused at the top of the stairs. "Hang on to me," she whispered, leading the way. From the bottom of the narrow stairs, they stumbled through the darkness to the kitchen.

At the back door, Morgan hung back. "Are you *sure* you know what you're doing?"

"Come *on,* before he gets away."

They stepped outside, and a frigid gust of wind sucked Alex's breath away. Morgan pulled the inside door closed with a click. Alex gripped her flip-flops with her toes and tiptoed to the corner to look around. The trash can under her window was covered, and Hutch had vanished.

"Where'd he go?" A muscle twitched in Alex's jaw.

"Look." Morgan pointed across the street. Down half a block, a dark figure passed in and out of shifting shadows.

"That's him. Why didn't he take his car? Too noisy? I bet he stashed drugs in *our* trash earlier, and now he's off to sell them!" Boy, were her grandparents in for a shock, Alex thought with satisfaction. Sweet old Hutch, the drug pusher.

Alex clutched her flapping shirt in one hand and pulled a protesting Morgan down the driveway with the other. Windwhipped hair stung her face. Their footsteps crunched on gravel, and Alex ignored the snow that got in her flip-flops.

"I'm freezing." Morgan tugged on Alex's arm. "How far do we have to follow him?"

"As far as we have to."

They tripped on cement edges sticking up in the sidewalk. The second time Alex stubbed her toe she realized her feet were growing numb. Goose bumps like small mountains covered her arms, and the bristles on her legs snagged her kitty pajamas as she strode along.

"Where is he?" Morgan pulled the comforter up around her face. "Let's turn around before we freeze."

While Alex started down the street, Hutch stepped out from between parked cars. "There." Alex kept her eyes glued to Hutch as she stepped off the curb. "Oh, shoot!" She gasped at the freezing puddle of water she'd stepped in. "Watch where you—"

But it was too late. Morgan stepped into another slushy puddle, slipping on the thin layer of ice that covered it. Flailing about, she reached for Alex, but the mummylike comforter was wrapped around her legs. She went down fast, splattering slushy water on Alex's bare ankles.

Alex bit back sharp words, then jerked Morgan to her feet and wiped off her own splattered legs. Turning, she spotted Hutch disappearing around a corner. "He's getting away!"

"I can't keep going. I'm frozen." Morgan sounded close to tears.

"Okay, wait for me at home. I may never get another good chance to nail Hutch." *Before escaping to Texas*, she added to herself.

"You can't wander around after midnight alone." Teeth chattering, Morgan held out the comforter. "Look. It's freezing."

Alex touched it. It was turning solid. "Just another block, okay? If I don't spot him then, we'll go back."

As Alex crossed the street this time, she kept her eyes carefully focused on the gutter. Then, without warning, a dark ball of fur streaked out from behind a privacy fence. A strangled *meereoow!* echoed behind it. Alex's heart nearly stopped, then thundered under her ribs. Before she could react, a snarling dog raced past, snapping at the cat's hindquarters.

Across the street, the cat leaped up a tree trunk. Underneath, the German shepherd barked loud enough to wake the dead.

Heart hammering, Alex grabbed Morgan's shoulder and nearly pushed her across the street. At the corner, Alex peered down Elm. Well lighted, that street held more expensive homes. She spotted Hutch more than a block away, near an estate with a brick wall surrounding its grounds.

Alex clenched her jaws to keep her own teeth from chattering. A sudden gust of wind blew swirling snow in her face. She turned her back to the wind, pulled her baggy shirt up to cover her face, then turned back around.

Hutch was gone.

"Come on! He's getting away!"

"I can't move any faster. My feet are frozen stumps."

Alex felt a momentary pang of guilt. Morgan's slushy comforter couldn't be any comfort now, the way it hung rigidly away from her legs. It—and her soggy tennis shoes—were freezing solid in the below-zero wind.

"Okay, you stand by that tree, out of the wind. I'll be right back."

Over Morgan's protests, she took off running. Her flip-flops slapped the sidewalk, and once she ran right out of one. Gasping as her bare foot hit the icy sidewalk, she backtracked and jammed it back on her numb foot.

By the time she reached the brick wall surrounding the grounds, Hutch was still nowhere in sight. Alex passed two locked, black wrought-iron gates. She stared inside at the big brick mansion. No movement there.

She trodded to where Morgan huddled against the tree. "I lost him." Alex peered up and down the deserted street. Lights only shone behind the windows of two homes. "Man, what a dead street."

"People with brains are in bed!" Morgan snapped. "Can we go now?"

"Sorry." Alex blinked at Morgan's outburst.

Trudging home, head bent against the howling wind, Alex felt stupid. *Talk about a wild-goose chase,* she thought. She'd have to swear Morgan to secrecy. In fact—

Without warning, a car's souped-up engine roared above the wind. Alex glanced up in time to see headlights bearing down on them as they crossed the street. Behind her, Morgan screamed a high-pitched wail. Flinging an arm across her eyes, Alex steeled her body against the impact.

Just then, the car screeched as it skidded to a halt just three feet away. Alex caught a whiff of burned rubber.

A car door opened. "Well, well, well," a laughing male voice said, "look at the cute kitty jammies."

Alex's knees threatened to buckle. *No! Oh, no, please, God! Not Ryan Thomas!*

But there was no mistaking the deep voice of Amber's popular older brother. Every girl Alex knew had a crush on him, although she found him as irritating as his sister.

"Hey, aren't you on the swim team?" he asked as he stepped closer.

Alex's lower lip shot out. "What's it to you?"

She clutched her shirt together, locked her shaking knees, and stretched herself to her full five feet, two inches. Head back, she linked her arm through Morgan's as if they were out for a pleasant Sunday stroll. Heat radiated up Alex's neck to her face. At least Ryan Thomas was good for one thing, she thought grimly. It was the first time she'd felt warm since they stepped outside.

"You little girls want a ride home? Your fingers are turning blue."

"I don't ride with maniacs who try to mow down innocent pedestrians." Tugging on Morgan's arm, Alex dragged her out of the headlights' glare.

"Suit yourself. Wait till the guys hear about this." Still laughing, he climbed back into his dual-exhaust car and roared off.

Alex hobbled stiffly toward home, fighting back tears of humiliation. The last thing she needed were tears freezing on her cheeks.

A block from home, when they passed beneath a tree, a soft *meow* drifted down. Alex gazed up through the bare branches. "Look. That cat's still up there. Here, kitty, kitty. You'll freeze up there."

Much to Alex's surprise, the cat carefully picked its way down, then jumped the last eight feet. Dark gray and white striped, had a wild look in its eyes. It circled Alex twice, purring and tickling her bare ankles.

"Poor kitty," she crooned, picking it up. The cat arched its back and jumped from Alex's arms, although it continued to purr. She examined its neck. "There's no tag. It must be a stray."

"Alex! I'm freezing!" Morgan turned and stomped away.

Alex hung back, lost in thought. She knew Hutch took in stray cats. It was one thing that Grandma thought was so wonderful about him. But come to think of it, Alex had never seen those cats again! What if Hutch experimented on them? Hutch didn't have a job either. *What if he ate the stray cats he took in?*

Squatting by the purring animal, Alex vowed that this was one stray cat Hutch would never touch. "Let's go. Kitty, kitty," she called, clomping along as fast as her numb feet would allow. The cat followed close on her heels.

Alex caught up with Morgan, and they stumbled down the driveway to the back door. Shivering, Alex scooped up the cat to smuggle into her room. "Open the door, okay? I've got the cat."

But Morgan turned slowly, her teeth chattering so hard Alex could barely understand her. "It's l-locked."

"It can't be." Alex shifted the cat to one arm, where it lay like a baby on its back. Alex reached out and twisted, then shook the door knob. Sure enough—it was locked.

Morgan's voice shook with emotion. "It must be a spring lock. They lock automatically when you close the door."

"That's just great." Alex glanced right, then left. "We'll just have to break in a basement window."

Just then the kitchen door flew open. "I wouldn't advise it," warned the low—and very angry—voice of Alex's grandfather.

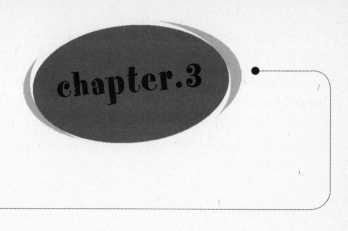

chapter.3

Alex clutched the cat and edged around her glaring grandfather. "We'd better get dry socks before our toes turn
black."

Grandpa McGee reached out and stopped Alex, but motioned
for Morgan to go upstairs. Morgan scooted out of the kitchen,
relief plain on her face. The cat struggled to get loose, and Alex set
it down on the braided rag rug.

Grandpa's eyebrows dipped into a scowl. "Now, kindly tell me
why you were sneaking outside after midnight, in your pajamas
no less."

Alex bristled at his tone. "Well, *your neighbor friend* woke us
up when he was yelling at his son. We looked out the window at
them, then saw this huge mean dog trap that poor cat in a tree.
We had to rescue it."

Her grandfather pointed one gnarled finger at her nose. "Alexandra, you may have been sneaking around town at all hours down in Texas, but I won't stand for it here. It's not *safe*. And stop spying on our neighbors. Their problems are none of your business." There was a hard glint in his eye. "You're as headstrong as your mother was. See where that landed her."

I'm not a baby! Alex wanted to scream. *Stop telling me what to do!*

"Go to bed after you put that cat outdoors."

"No, it needs me. I'll keep it in my room." Alex bit her lower lip. "Please."

"Just for tonight then." Without another word, he left the room.

Alex shivered as she opened a can of tuna. Reaching down for the cat, she suddenly wondered what she'd do if nature called. She needed a litterbox for her room.

"Okay, kitty, till tomorrow, control yourself."

By the time she got up to her room with the cat and tuna, Alex had some tingling feelings back in her fingers and toes. The blast of hot air from her heater felt like heaven. Morgan was already in bed, blankets pulled up to her nose. Her wet pajamas and soggy comforter lay in a pile by the closet door.

"Are you thawing out yet?" Alex suddenly felt guilty about nearly freezing Morgan to death.

"Some. Is your grandpa le-le-letting you kee-kee-keep the cat?"

"'Just for tonight,'" she mimicked his gruff voice. "Grandma will talk him into it tomorrow, though." She put the cat and food on the floor, but the cat strutted from one side of the room to the other before sticking its nose in the bowl. "Morgan, meet Maverick."

Morgan leaned up on one elbow to study the cat. "Why M-Maverick?"

"It fits." Alex searched the room for a place for the cat to sleep. "In Texas a maverick is a wild independent animal. That cat seems pretty independent."

"You have wild cats down there?"

"No. A guy named Sam Maverick from Galveston Island had *cattle* that were kinda wild. They wouldn't travel with the herd, and wranglers called 'em mavericks." *Kinda like me,* Alex thought. She'd always prided herself on refusing to travel with the herd. This cat seemed just like her. "I know where it can sleep," Alex said, snapping her fingers.

She hadn't brought enough clothes from Texas to fill all the dresser drawers. The bottom drawer only held a faded purple sweatshirt she didn't wear anymore. She spread it out. Instant cat bed!

"Alex, look!" Morgan cried.

Alex turned and laughed out loud. There, sitting in front of the computer's screen saver, was Maverick. Perfectly still except for a twitching tail, it watched the bright orange computerized fish swim back and forth across the screen. "At least my *mouse* won't appeal to her!"

Alex nudged the cat down, then logged on to the TodaysGirls.com chat room to see if Amber was there, and if so, whether her brother had gone home and reported seeing Morgan and her in their pajamas. The right-hand column listed faithful1 and nycbutterfly.

faithful1: Hey Alex. WB. Wuzzup?

TX2step: getting ready 2 crash. Morgan's catching zzzzz's already.

nycbutterfly: that's my baby sister!

faithful1: back to biology . . . I got Tim 4 a lab partner. ACK! I know he's not going 2 get any work done.

nycbutterfly: But did U C those jeans he had on today? Hold me back!

faithful1: LOL! Alex, what did you guys do tonight?

Alex stiffened. Was that a trick question? Had Ryan come home and told Amber what happened? Feeling the heat crawling up her neck, Alex decided to bluff it out.

TX2step: Watched a video and a basketball game on TV.

nycbutterfly: Basketball, ugh. Can u believe that unit in PE is finally over?

faithful1: No, but guess what's next? Square dancing!

nycbutterfly: I can't believe schools r required 2 teach dancing. I hope I don't get stuck w/Jon, he kinda smells.

TX2step: Gotta catch some zzzz's myself. CUL8R

Alex clicked the *Exit* button and the screen disappeared. *So far, so good,* she thought as she crawled into bed. Minutes later, she drifted off to sleep with Ryan Thomas's laughter in her ears . . .

Alex awoke the next morning, spitting and coughing. "Get off me!" She pushed the cat away from her face and glanced at her clock. "Almost time to get up for church anyway. Want some toast or something?"

"Sure." Morgan threw off the covers to reveal yesterday's school clothes, now wrinkled and twisted.

"Oh man, *look*." Alex pinched her nose and pointed to a mess in the bottom dresser drawer. A stinky brown pile sat right in the middle of the clean sweatshirt.

"Guess your cat made its own litter box."

"Very funny." Alex opened the window for fresh air, then folded up the sweatshirt. "This is going straight in the garbage can."

Outside a moment later, Alex threw away the shirt and studied the house next door. After last night, she knew Hutch was up to no good, but she needed help to prove it. Then she remembered her grandma's Neighborhood Watch group, organized after a vacationing neighbor was burglarized. Alex had helped her grandmother put the group on a list serve to e-mail them notices. She could use that e-mail list for her own purposes.

Inside, while Morgan tempted Maverick with some bits of

toast, Alex hunted in the basement and filled an old dishpan with potting soil. Until she got some kitty litter, that should do.

Back in her bedroom, Alex first checked her e-mail. Her heart beat faster when she saw a message was loading. Maybe her mom—! But when it popped up, she recognized the sender's e-mail address: Grandma.

Once Grandma had understood e-mail, she'd started sending little poems to her friends and neighbors several times a week. She put Alex on her list, too. Even though Alex thought the poems were sappy, they had an odd way of landing in her mailbox when she really needed one. This one read:

It's So Easy

It's always so easy to feel all alone,
To think no one else knows the heartache you've known.
It's easy to look in the mirror and see
A person whose luck is as bad as can be.

Alex stared at the screen, open-mouthed. It was as if her grandmother had read her mind.

How easy it is to forget what we've got,
To dwell almost always on what we have *not*.
But practicing how to be thankful for things
Makes it easy to face life and all that it brings.

If only it were that easy, Alex thought, clicking the *New Message* button. In the address line, she typed "Neighborhood Watch." She double-checked to make sure Hutch wasn't on the list yet, then typed a short message.

Does anyone have information on the new neighbor who calls himself Hutch? Seen any suspicious activity? Have noticed odd late-night behavior. PLEASE FORWARD this question to your friends, then get back to me.

Alex clicked *Send.* She'd show her grandfather what his wonderful neighbor was up to, and she bet it wouldn't take long to find out.

"What're you doing?" Morgan popped into the room, dressed now in black pants and a green sweater.

"Testing a hunch. I'll tell you later." She nudged the cat off her lap. "I'd better see if the bathroom's free."

She met her grandmother out in the hall. In her bright yellow church dress, she looked like a lemon on legs. "Thanks for the poem just now," Alex said.

Grandma's forehead wrinkled even more than usual. "I didn't send anything this morning."

"Really? The date said today."

"Emily?" Grandpa called from their bedroom. "I saw you coming out of Alex's room earlier. Are you sure you didn't send some e-mail?"

"But I wasn't in Alex's room this morning."

"You really don't remember?"

Alex was surprised at the worried tone in her grandfather's voice. Old people forgot stuff all the time. What was the big deal? She hurried away to get dressed for church.

However, at church Alex felt edgy. It was just one more place where she didn't belong. She really wouldn't mind the whole church thing if the place wasn't full of hypocrites like her grumpy grandfather. Miss Perfect Amber attended church there, too, and Alex spotted Morgan's sister, Maya, with her. Jamie and Coach Short went there, too, but Alex couldn't spot them anywhere.

Morgan elbowed her in the ribs. "Look who just walked in."

Alex spotted a cleaned-up Hutch at the back of the church, shaking hands with her grandparents. "Come on." Alex waved to Amber and Maya, but kept one eye on Hutch as she headed his way.

"Bonjour, ma cherie." Amber slipped an arm through Morgan's. "Just who I wanted to see!"

"Sorry. No *parlez-vous Français* here."

"No problem. You can sign up in plain English."

"For what?" Alex asked, straining to catch Hutch's words behind her.

"In Sunday school we planned that show we told you about for next weekend. There's still time for you two to enter. Maybe a song and dance routine?"

"Oh, sure." *Spend my weekend displaying my lack of talent? I don't think so.* Turning, she ran into Coach Short.

"Say there, Alex," Coach said, handing her a bulletin, "don't forget about tomorrow. I'll pick you up at ten till five."

Alex groaned, but didn't argue. "Sure. Thanks." She might as well play along till she ran away. Still, practicing at 5:00 A.M. was stupid. She didn't need it. Nobody could beat her freestyle record.

"—tough finding a job," Hutch was saying directly behind Alex, "but there's a good opening in today's paper." She listened hard while pretending to read her bulletin.

"That's so difficult." Sympathy oozed out of her grandmother's voice. "Jobs are scarce this time of year."

"Can we help out in the meantime?" Grandpa asked.

Alex tensed. Help him out? How?

Hutch cleared his throat. "I hate to ask, but a small loan would help. Just a little something till a job turns up—"

The organist started playing then and drowned him out. People drifted away, and Alex fumed all the way down the aisle to their pew. That skunk Hutch was hitting up her retired grandparents for a loan! That good-for-nothing. And Grandpa had the nerve to criticize Alex's dad for not always working.

"What's eating you?" Morgan whispered when they slid into the pew.

"I overheard Hutch weasling my grandparents out of a loan just now. Good grief! They're on Social Security. What a crook."

"Maybe you're being too suspicious. I mean—"

"Not you, too! Look, Morgan." Alex dropped her voice when the organ paused between hymns. "I am about the most open-minded person I know. I'm just not naive. I don't judge people without good reason, not like Grandpa." She glanced over her shoulder; her grandparents were heading up the aisle, with Hutch right behind them.

"Alex, you are so narrow-minded, you could look through a keyhole with both eyes at the same time," Morgan laughed, quickly covering her mouth.

"It's not judgmental to be honest!" Alex snapped.

All through the church service, Alex sat with shoulders hunched and head down, letting her hair hide the fact that she was dozing. She jerked awake when the organist opened up all the stops for one hymn, but she barely mouthed the words about an ever-present God. If God was there, Alex sure couldn't feel him.

She slumped farther down in the pew, willing the service to be over . . .

A few minutes later Morgan nudged her awake. Alex yawned and glanced down to the end of the pew. Coach was handing Hutch the offering plate. Hutch dropped in a bill, then smiled at Grandma as he passed the plate to her.

"Hypocrite," Alex muttered.

"Shhh!" Morgan shook her head at her.

"All I can say is, they'd better watch Hutch. He'd take money *out* of the offering instead of putting some *in*."

Grandpa cleared his throat, and his warning was clear. *Well, fine*, she thought, slouching back down in the pew. *Let that crook steal the church's money. See if I care.*

At the end of the service, right in front of Morgan, Alex's grandfather turned to her. "One more display like that during church and I will personally take you out of here. Next week you will look alert and be quiet. And you'll find something to wear to church besides old clothes big enough for an elephant." He gripped the back of the pew ahead of them. "Alexandra, if you weren't out running around town half the night, you wouldn't have trouble staying awake in church."

Heat rushed up Alex's neck and spread to her face, where it radiated out from her in waves. She thought she'd die. He'd treated her like a three-year-old!

Fine! Alex thought, keeping her eyes on the floor. He wouldn't have to worry about her next week. She wouldn't **be** there next week!

Morgan tapped Alex on the shoulder. "Um, I'm supposed to go home with Maya."

"Sure." Alex couldn't look up. The last thing she wanted to see on Morgan's face was sympathy.

Through eyes narrowed to slits, Alex watched her grandparents work their way down the center aisle to the double doors at the back. Every few steps they stopped and talked to someone.

It made her sick watching her grandfather smile and shake hands with people after he'd just humiliated her. And in church, no less!

Alex glanced over her shoulder. There must be other ways out of the building than through the double front doors. She strode up the aisle toward the altar and quickly darted into the choir room.

There, she ran down a short flight of steps to an outside door. With her hand on the knob, a thought struck Alex so hard that she stumbled. *She didn't have to wait till the end of the month to run home to Texas. She could do it right now.*

Alex had kept her jacket on, and she had five dollars in her pocket. Enough for some snacks. Outside, she blinked at the glare off the snow, then turned away from the parking lot. She knew where Highway 27 headed out of town. She'd jog there, pick up a ride, and head south. She'd shake the snow from this town off her shoes and—

Without warning, a heavy hand gripped her shoulder. Hard.

Alex spun around, jerking loose at the same time. The hand gripped harder. "Ow! Let go of me!"

Hutch dropped his hand. "Sorry. I didn't mean to hurt you." He leaned so close that Alex could see the red veins in his eyes. "Where are you off to in such a hurry?"

"What business is it of yours?"

"None. I'm just concerned. You looked upset." He swept a shock of brown hair from his eye, then bent close. "Hitchhiking is dangerous."

Alex's mouth dropped open. How could he know what she'd planned to do?

Just then her grandfather's voice boomed across the parking lot. "Alexandra! Time to head home."

For a long moment, Alex stared at Hutch, feeling like a caged animal. Then, shoulders sagging, she turned around and headed back toward her grandfather's car.

chapter.4

At home, Grandpa headed for his recliner with the Sunday paper while Grandma tested the meat loaf and baked potatoes in the oven. "Mmmm, almost done." She then took lettuce and tomatoes from the vegetable crisper. "We'll eat in fifteen minutes. Would you set the table, Alex?"

Still stinging from her encounters with both her grandfather and Hutch at church, Alex yanked open the cupboard door. Meat loaf again. *Ugh.* "Grandma, don't you wish you could afford to eat out for Sunday dinner?" *With the money you give that phony crook next door, you could afford to.*

"Heavens, no. I've cooked Sunday dinner for your grandfather for over fifty years. It's one of my favorite things to do." She reached over to rinse off a tomato. "Anyway, with his high blood pressure, I can be sure his food isn't filled with salt."

"If you didn't give away so much money . . ." Alex let her hint hang in the air. That was something she'd *never* understand, giving away all that money. Heaven knows, her grandparents needed it themselves.

Grandma handed Alex the salad and dressing. "I just trust God to take care of us. He says that if he can take care of the birds of the air and the flowers, he'll take even better care of us."

Biting her tongue with great effort, Alex pivoted on her heel and marched to the dining room. How could anyone live to Grandma's age, yet be so simpleminded? Didn't Grandma know that, in this world, you had to look out for yourself because no one else would? Isn't that why God gave them brains? Alex didn't need God; she didn't need anybody. Anyway, if her own dad didn't care enough to look out for her, how could she expect some invisible heavenly Father to do it?

"Dinner's ready!" Grandma called, setting the meat loaf on the table.

A minute later, Alex fumed silently while her grandfather said grace. *He doesn't just say grace either,* Alex thought, *he intones grace.* Suddenly exhausted, she reached for the salt and pepper to doctor up her food.

Head bent over her plate, Alex was careful not to meet her grandfather's eye. She still burned from his treatment at church. If only she were hitchhiking to Texas right now instead of choking down Grandma's bland meat loaf. *I'll get that nosy*

Hutch, she thought grimly. Some day—and soon—she'd make him pay.

She needed to sit down and carefully plan her escape. The next time she ran, no one would see—or stop—her.

"Aren't you hungry?" Grandma asked, interrupting her thoughts.

Alex pushed the mushy meat loaf around her plate. "Not really," she said. *Not for this junk anyway,* she thought. "I had a big breakfast."

More than anything sometimes, Alex missed the food from home. The so-called Mexican food up north was a joke! She'd nearly gagged when she'd ordered a taco at the Gnosh Pit. Talk about cardboard. She missed spicy Mexican food cooked by people who knew an enchilada from a tamale. She nearly drooled as she recalled the rellanos at the Cactus Cookoff she'd attended every fall.

"Do you have plans with Morgan today?" Grandma asked.

"No, not yet. I'll see if she's in the chat room later and ask her."

Grandpa leaned back from the table, unbuttoning his bottom vest button. "In your mother's day, Sunday was reserved for families to be together. She didn't have friends over."

Alex still stung from his tongue-lashing at church. "Maybe Mom ran away from all that *togetherness.*" She shoved back her chair and ran up to her room.

Still fuming, Alex logged on, found the chat room, and

scanned the list on the right. She hoped Morgan was there, but only Jamie and Bren were logged on.

> rembrandt: good to c u, Alex!
> TX2step: just putting off doing homework
> chicChick: I hear u! I really don't want 2 study 2day, but
> I can't afford another bad grade. I need help!
> rembrandt: hey, check this out. Found it last nite. Great
> homework helper site @ www.homeworkcentral.com
> chicChick: how's it work?
> rembrandt: not sure. just found it.
> TX2step: I've used it B4. They have an ask-the-editor
> section. u just ask them stuff & they'll email u
> information.
> chicChick: Straight from heaven!
> TX2step: wish I could use it 2day. Have 2 write a poem.
> YUK. Gotta go. Homework calling my name. CU

Alex exited, then pushed back her chair. In a daze, she tripped over the comforter, now dry, in a heap on the floor. She folded it to put away in the closet, but even stretching to her full height, she could barely reach the bottom shelf. She jumped up, but in the process knocked against a cardboard box.

The box fell, landing upside down. "Oh, man." Alex dropped to her knees. When she turned the box over, several horse books, a doll, some doll clothes, and a chess game fell out. Alex realized it was a collection of her mom's childhood toys.

As she handled her mom's old playthings, Alex felt a closeness to her that had been missing for weeks. While Alex refolded doll clothes, Maverick pushed her furry face through the crook in Alex's arm, her whiskers twitching. Alex laughed and pulled Maverick onto her lap, but the cat squirmed over on her back to bat at Alex's fingers.

"Wait!" Alex reached for the doll's bonnet. "Here, I've got a pretty hat for you, now that we know you're a girl."

Surprisingly, Maverick allowed Alex to put the bonnet on her and even tie it under the cat's chin. Alex crooned a lullaby, surprised that she even knew the words to such a song. Then, without warning, overwhelming feelings of sadness engulfed her.

Bent over, Alex sat perfectly still, waiting for the burning pain in her chest to pass, but it didn't. Instead, her throat seemed to swell shut, and her vision blurred. Suddenly she was no longer holding Maverick in a baby bonnet. Instead, it was seven years ago, and Alex cuddled her baby sister in her arms . . .

Alex had been seven the year Emmy died. Crib death, the doctor had diagnosed, and no one's fault.

She'd never believed the doctor. After all, Emmy was left in her care while Mom brought Dad home from a bar that night. Several years after Emmy's death, Alex had seen a TV special about crib death. Doctors claimed it could be prevented if babies were put to bed on their backs instead of their stomachs.

Alex had known ever since then that putting her baby sister to sleep on her stomach had caused her death.

Tears seeped from beneath her eyelashes, ran down, and dripped off her chin.

What would her life have been like, Alex wondered, if her sister had lived? Emmy, named for Grandma Emily, would have been eight now. They could have leaned on each other and taken care of their parents together. Alex would have given anything for that. Sometimes, she hated to admit, the job was too big for her alone.

Monday morning Alex was up before her alarm, which was set at 4:30. She logged online and waited. The little green arrow popped up. She had mail! Alex's heart raced as she watched the computer load seven messages. At last! Surely now she'd find out why her mom had been silent lately.

When the messages were loaded, however, none were from her mom. Alex's stomach cramped. *What was going on at home?*

Alex glanced at the clock, then opened the mail. Six messages were responses from her inquiry about Hutch. Three people knew nothing at all, but said they'd forward her message. The other three people lived on this block and the next. They'd noticed the same things Alex mentioned: Hutch's irregular hours, no apparent job, poking through trash cans. Two of them also mentioned his car's broken muffler.

No real news yet, Alex thought, but she bet something would turn up soon. With this many pairs of eyes pinned on him, old

Hutch would get nailed good. She smiled grimly. She couldn't wait to see her grandfather's face when his precious neighbor turned out to be a criminal.

The last e-mail was from her grandmother. She scanned the list of addresses, looking for Hutch's. Sure enough, there it was:

peace60s@aol.com.

She read Grandma's message quickly:

Count

Count your blessings instead of your crosses,
Count your gains instead of your losses.

Count your joys instead of your woes,
Count your friends instead of your foes.

Count your smiles instead of your tears,
Count your courage instead of your fears.

Alex sighed. If only she had her grandma's simple life, where advice like this poem actually worked.

After closing down her browser, Alex glanced at her alarm clock and scrambled into her clothes. Coach Short would be there in ten minutes. She scooped her lunch money off her dresser to jam in her pocket, then reconsidered.

She'd better save every penny she had, she decided. It'd be safer to buy a bus ticket to Texas instead of hitchhiking. About that *one thing*, she figured Hutch was right. Hitchhiking was dangerous. If she skipped meals and saved this month's lunch ticket money, that was thirty dollars right there.

Alex glanced out her bedroom window as headlights swung into her driveway. Grabbing her bags, she headed downstairs.

Outside she climbed into the front seat of Coach's minivan. Coach lived just two blocks away, so she got picked up first. "Glad you could make it today" was all he said as he backed out.

"Mmmm." Alex huddled down inside her coat. The van was toasty already, blasting hot air on her feet and legs. Instant drowsy.

She closed her eyes, grateful to be near the heater. Actually, Morgan had quietly informed her months ago that the front seat next to Coach was reserved for Amber. Alex had never heard of anything so stupid. It was "first come, first serve," and Miss Perfect could deal with it. Who elected Amber the pope anyway?

Coach Short broke into her reverie as he pulled onto Jackson Street, where Morgan and Maya lived. "Before we pick up the others, I wanted to ask . . . how are things with you?"

Alex stretched her head up out of her collar, like a turtle emerging from its shell. "Everything's cool." In the light from the dash, she tried to read Coach's expression. What was he really asking? Had Hutch squealed about their conversation outside the church yesterday?

"You've missed several practices. Sure you're okay?" Eyes

straight ahead, he turned into Morgan's driveway. His headlights swept briefly across her two-story, colonial brick home.

Stretching casually, Alex studied Coach's profile. He was fishing for something, but what? What had he heard? What had he guessed? "I'm fine. No problems. Really."

"Then you need to be at practices from now on. You're part of the team, and you let everyone down when you skip. Amber's been swimming freestyle for the relay practices, but it's not her job to fill in for you. She has her own events to train for."

Alex fumed as she watched the side window fog over. Miss Perfect strikes again! "Sorry." Like Amber could ever take her place! Amber swam the *back*stroke, for Pete's sake, with her face out of the water. Had Coach forgotten Alex had held the freestyle record in Texas for two years? Even if she just showed up for the meets, she'd still leave the competition in her wake.

Just then Maya and Morgan emerged from the side of the house, both puffy-looking in down-filled winter jackets. Maya yanked open the van's side door, tossed her gym bag on the floor, and crawled in. "Hi, everybody."

Morgan followed, slamming the door behind her. "'Morning," she said, yawning so wide Alex heard her jaws pop. "Brrr! Send some heat back here, please. I've been cold *all weekend.*"

Holding her breath, Alex aimed the vent to the back. Was Morgan going to reveal their Saturday night escapade into the great frozen outdoors?

Apparently not, Alex finally decided after they picked up Jamie, then Amber.

"Hey, you guys," Amber said, crawling into the back, "you like my new jeans? I bought them at a great sale at the mall yesterday."

"Really cute!" Jamie said.

"Yeah," Maya agreed, "there were good sales at the Gap, too. I got some cute shirts."

Who cares? Alex thought, looking down at her worn jeans. *Mondays are enough of a royal pain,* she thought as she slid down on her tailbone, *without a 5:00 A.M. swim practice and listening to this stupid chatter.*

But ten minutes later, as she tugged on her red tank suit and inhaled the steamy chlorine pool smell, Alex admitted to herself how much she'd missed swimming.

A shrill whistle blast echoed in the cavernous room. "Gather round," Coach yelled. "Okay, the big meet's tomorrow with Drake, and I'm not happy with some of your times. Since Alex has graced us with her presence today, let's start with your relay team."

Alex stared at the whistle resting on Coach's ample stomach. Was that his idea of a joke? Well, she'd show them. She'd pour it on this morning, making her time even *better* than before.

"To warm up, I want Alex and Amber in a practice freestyle. Jamie, time Alex. I want to know how hard to work her today."

"Yes, sir, Coach, sir." Jamie grinned at Alex and swung the stopwatch at her.

Alex pulled on her cap, tucked in her curly ends, and slipped into the pool. "Ready?" Coach called when Amber jumped in beside her.

Amber flexed her shoulders. "Glad you're back. We missed you."

Alex mumbled, "Thanks" but didn't know whether to believe her or not. Amber was too nicey-nice to be trusted sometimes. "Don't forget to come up for air," Alex said. "Remember, this isn't the backstroke."

Leaning forward in her starting position, Alex tensed as she waited for the Coach's whistle. She'd show him. When the shrill blast came, she pushed off hard and shot forward in her lane. Amber was on her back side, but Alex could hear her churning right along beside her. Well, she'd show Amber, too. Just because Miss Perfect had filled in for her the past week didn't mean anything.

By the time Alex reached the far end of the pool, her legs already ached and her chest hurt. She wasn't worried, though. By the end of the morning practice, she'd be 100 percent. When she turned to head back down her lane, she was mildly surprised to see Amber swimming with her neck and neck.

Ignoring the cramp forming in her side, Alex pushed harder. No way was she willing to beat Amber by just a few strokes. It was time to lengthen her lead or she'd never hear the end of it from Coach.

Halfway down the length of the pool, however, the cramp in her side worsened. Alex continued to push hard, gulping air like a distressed fish. Heading this direction, Amber was in her line of vision, and with horror, Alex watched her pull away.

Soon Alex was looking at Amber's kicking feet, then even her feet disappeared.

Amber finished the freestyle race a good four yards ahead of Alex. Alex finally touched the end of the pool, grabbing the side with one hand and her ribs with the other. She jerked when Amber touched her shoulder.

"Don't worry. You'll be in top form for the meet tomorrow."

Alex shook off her hand and fought back tears of frustration. To be beaten in her own event—and by *Amber*, no less. It was totally degrading.

She dragged herself out of the pool and glared defiantly at Coach Harry. She refused to ask what her time had been. She pulled off her cap and shook out her long curls.

"This is what I was afraid of." Coach turned in a slow circle, meeting each girl's eye. "Let this be a lesson to you all. Consistency with practices is our key to winning."

Alex clenched her jaw and stared at the trail of wet footprints crisscrossing the cement floor. This was the *third* lecture she'd endured publicly in two days. First her grandfather and Hutch, and now Coach. It was too much. It was just too much.

When Coach stopped talking, she lifted her eyes and stared in the direction of his chin. "Since Amber's so great in my spot, she can have it." She threw her cap down on the wet cement. "I quit. Comprende?"

A collective gasp arose from the rest of her relay team. "Alex, no!" Morgan said. "You don't mean that."

"Oh, don't I?" Chin up and pushed forward, she marched into the locker room. What was the point in practicing anyway? She was heading to Texas as soon as she had a bus ticket. Coach would have to replace her on the team soon anyway.

In the shower room, she had her choice of stalls. No more waiting till all the upper classmen showered. Alex turned on the hot water full force. Quitting was one way to get around those stupid rules.

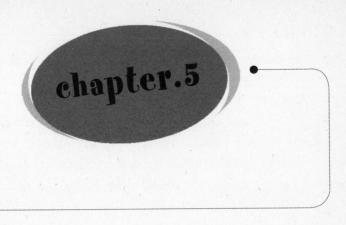

chapter.5

W ell, look what the cat dragged in." Eyes deep-set and brooding under heavy brows, Matthew stared at Alex's frizzy hair.

Alex slouched in her seat next to him in the computer lab. "What a compliment. I'm all choked up." She knew her hair was drying wild, but Matthew had a lot of nerve. Resembling a "before" picture for a shampoo commercial, *his* hair hung in hunks, tucked behind ears with silver, barbed earrings that looked tarnished. His fingernails even had grease under them. "Don't you know grime alters the taste of finger foods?" she asked sweetly.

"You're a strain on the eyes, Tex."

"Like *your* appearance brightens *my* day?" she snapped.

Matthew raised an eyebrow, the pierced one. "Maybe you could loan me your Alamo shirt to brighten my wardrobe."

Her eyes slid over his perpetual black shirt and jeans. "I've known armadillos with more style."

"Stall? What's *stall*?"

Alex gritted her teeth. What nerve that creep had, making fun of her accent and her clothes. Anyway, she loved her Alamo shirt, a souvenir from one of the few fun trips with her family.

"Maybe I wouldn't look like something the cat dragged in if I got enough sleep." She tilted her head back and looked down her nose at his acne-scarred face. "You see, I have these weird neighbors who fight outside in the middle of the night. Interesting view from my window, your dad spread over the hood of the car."

Matthew's upper lip curled back to reveal fanglike eyeteeth, perfect for a werewolf movie. "You Nazi spy."

"Like it's *my* fault your dad goes through garbage cans. Is that where he finds your clothes?"

Matthew flushed a dark mottled red.

"You shut up!" He growled like a mean, hungry dog, then turned back to his own computer, which Alex noticed was set on WebCrawler. What weird thing was he searching for today? How to clone vampire bats?

Moving her chair sideways, she turned her back on Matthew, determined to focus on something positive in this lousy day. *Great idea*, Alex thought sourly, except there was nothing positive in her life. All that appealed to her was her dream of escaping.

Well, then, that's what I'll do in lab today, she thought.

Ignoring the muttering scruffy hulk beside her, Alex found her bookmarked Ask Jeeves search engine. *"Where can I find bus schedules?"* she typed in the box. Thanks to the fiber-optic lines in the school, this computer loaded ten times faster than Grandma's old one. In just seconds, Jeeves offered her ten choices. She clicked on the Greyhound Fare Finder. In the drop-down box titled "Select Origin State," she chose Indiana, then typed "Edgewood," and clicked *Continue.*

Under "Select Destination," she clicked Burnet in the Texas file. Dates, times, and prices filled the screen. Pencil in hand, she copied down the information.

The local Greyhound station listed daily trips, leaving for Texas at 11:15 A.M. and 8:40 P.M., with arrival the next day. Both times cost the same price: $125 one-way for an adult ticket.

Now came the question of the century: Where would she get $125? She'd have to skip a lot of lunches—like about four months' worth—to save that. No way was she waiting that long to leave! She'd have to find another source of income, and soon.

By lunchtime, she was past hunger but had a splitting headache from skipping breakfast before practice. She had no desire to see anyone, yet Edgewood High had a closed campus. They were required to go to the cafeteria, whether they ate or not.

In the cafeteria, Alex headed across the echoing room toward an individual study table along the north window. She'd hole up and ignore everybody. She was halfway there when Morgan's voice rang out.

"Alex! Over here!"

Alex paused, closed her eyes, then pivoted in the direction of Morgan's voice. Morgan and Jamie Chandler lounged at their usual table near the à la carte line. After quitting the team that morning, the last thing Alex needed was another lecture. But Morgan was smiling and pointing to a vacant chair.

The smell of spaghetti and coffeecake had Alex drooling by the time she sat down. Morgan looked fine, but Jamie stared at her plate as she twirled spaghetti on her fork. *Guess she has a problem with my quitting,* Alex thought. *Well, so what?* None of them understood her. Mostly they lived in expensive homes with both parents. Jamie wasn't rich, but she still had her real mom and her home. That's all Alex wanted.

"Aren't you eating?" Morgan asked. She dipped a carrot stick into ranch dressing, licked it off, then re-dipped it.

"Not hungry today," Alex said, knowing she'd give her right arm for some hot Texas chili or spicy hush puppies.

"You sure? Want some of mine?"

"Nope." Alex tried to smooth down her fluffy hair by sticking it behind her ears.

Morgan waved her fork at her. "I have some spray in my bag that helps control frizzies, if you want to use it."

"Doubt if it would help." Alex had tried to comb it in the

bathroom, but gave up. It resembled a thorny cactus more than a head of hair.

Just then Amber and Maya pushed through a group at the snack line and headed their way. Alex wanted to crawl under the table. After being beaten in her own race, Amber was the last person Alex wanted to see.

Almost the last person, Alex corrected herself, catching a glimpse of Ryan Thomas, horsing around and punching another basketball player in the arm. *Please, God, don't let him see me.* She slouched down in her seat.

Amber set her tray down opposite Alex. "I can't believe I'm eating this." She lifted her hamburger bun and poked at the meat. "Look at all this grease."

Nobody responded to Amber's effort at conversation. The tension was so thick among the swim team members that Alex thought she might suffocate. She never should have chosen their lunch table.

Just then Morgan, with her mouth full of spaghetti, whimpered and pinched her nose. Grabbing her napkin, she was only half successful in covering her mouth before erupting into an explosive sneeze. Strings of spaghetti and red sauce splattered across the table.

"Ew! Gross, Morgan!"

"I'm sorry!" Morgan grabbed Amber's napkin and her own to wipe up the mess. Jamie and Maya giggled, breaking the tension.

"Really, Morgan, I said that I didn't want any of your

spaghetti." Alex laughed and dabbed at the red sauce on her backpack. When she glanced up, she groaned inwardly. Ryan Thomas was headed toward their table. Alex quickly dropped her paper napkin on the floor, then bent over as if to retrieve it. *Don't let him see me*, Alex prayed. But when she sat back up, he was standing by his sister.

"Hey, Amber, you got any change?" Ryan asked, his voice husky.

Jamie, Maya, and Morgan all gazed up at the popular basketball senior. Dimples appeared on both sides of Jamie's mouth. Alex looked away and stared out a window.

"What for?" Amber took a slurp of Dr. Pepper.

"I gotta go to vendoland. Hand it over."

"Sorry, don't have any."

Ryan ruffled Amber's hair, then grinned at the girls gazing up at him. His eyes stopped on Alex. He grinned even wider and winked. "Looks like you made it home all right."

Amber, Maya, and Jamie glanced at Alex. Jamie jabbed her on the leg. "What's he talking about?"

Ryan grabbed two of Amber's French fries. "I nearly ran over her Saturday night." He dipped the fries in his sister's ketchup, then stuffed them in his mouth. "Bet I'm the only guy who's seen you in those hot pajamas!" Laughing, he turned and strutted away, leaving three girls staring after him.

"You guys," Amber said, "it's just my brother." They heaved a collective sigh, blinked, and turned back around.

"Do you think he'll come to the next swim meet?" Morgan's smile vanished, replaced by a look of near agony. "I mean, we got those new red suits."

Maya whistled through the tiny gap in her front teeth.

Oh barf, Alex thought.

Maya turned to Alex. "I'm *much more interested* in where he saw you in your pj's! What was he talking about?"

Alex forced herself to shrug. Then the bell rang, and she was spared answering. Banging shoulders with other students, Alex lengthened her stride as they funneled out the cafeteria door, leaving her friends and their questions behind.

Turning the corner, Alex trudged off to health. She hated health. Their teacher, Ms. Shafer, was the Queen of Group Projects. Supposedly these projects taught them how to work together. *Yeah, right*, Alex thought. It really taught the lazy pigs like Gnarly Karl and Holly Hippo Hips to be lazier, while people like her got stuck with all the work.

The only thing she hated worse about health class today was the fact that Matthew was in it.

She slunk into class, hoping to appear invisible. No such luck.

"*Hisss!* How's our favorite rattlesnake from the deep South?"

"Shut up, Karl." Dropping her bags on the floor, Alex kicked them under her chair and slumped into her seat.

"Don't tell me to shut up." Karl loomed over her, his hands as big as hams as he leaned on her desk. "*Y'all* could be a lot friendlier to old Karl."

Alex wanted nothing more than to kick Karl in the shins, but Ms. Shafer could be heard in the hall. Anyway, Karl outweighed her by fifty pounds and was a full foot taller. Alex would never have admitted to anyone—she could barely stand to admit it to herself—but Karl terrified her.

"Hey, I'm talking to you!" He slapped his hands hard on her desk and snorted when she jumped. "Remember the Alamo, *y'all*!" After bowing at the smattering of applause, he swaggered to his seat as Ms. Shafer floated into the room.

Alex glared at his broad back, then happened to glance to her left. Two rows over, Matthew sneered at her.

Man, get me out of this jail, Alex thought. She closed her eyes and visualized climbing aboard a Greyhound bus bound for Texas. The scenery rolling by would transform from dirty slushy snow, to winding bubbly streams, to red flowering trees, to blue swimming pools and waving green grass and—

The teacher's voice snapped her back to reality. "—and of course, the laws of heredity." She surveyed the room with eyes defined by a layer of false lashes. "Who read their chapter and can explain to the class about Gregor Mendel's plant hybrid experiments?"

She glanced quizzically at Alex, who promptly stared at her hands and picked her cuticles. Any half-wit would know who Mendel was, but she refused to raise her hand. She got too much attention as it was.

"Alex? Do you know?"

Alex sighed and ignored Karl's snicker. "Mendel was an Austrian monk who first did experiments with plant genes." Her tone was flat. "He used garden peas."

"That's right!" Ms. Shafer beamed, as if Alex had recited the Constitution word for word. Chattering nonstop, the teacher drew graphs and charts on her overhead, illustrating blossom color in peas, of all things. Alex stared at her book without seeing it, willing the class to be over and growing drowsier by the minute.

However, a question from the back of the room caught her attention and made her sit up. "I don't understand," Matthew said. "What about traits like violence or alcoholism? Doctors now say that these are inherited traits."

Alex studied Matthew out of the corner of her eye. Something smelled fishy. Matthew never talked in class.

"Studies do indicate this." Ms. Shafer patted her sparse blonde hair, harshly bleached.

"If it's inherited, then you can't help it, right?" Matthew frowned. "So why go to AA to treat alcoholism, if it's in your genes?"

"Excellent question! Geneticists and behavior psychologists don't agree on this, I'm afraid." Ms. Shafer spoke in nasal tones as if she were pinching her nose. "Even if you have an alcoholic parent, that doesn't mean you'll be one, too."

"Would it be the same all over the country?" Matthew asked.

"I'm not sure I understand your question."

"Well, is there a higher concentration of violence in the North, like New York City? Do gang-member fathers have gang member kids? Or do kids born in Houston become alcoholics because their dads are drunks?"

Alex's head snapped around, and she stared at Matthew. Kids born in Houston? *She'd* been born in Houston, and her dad was an alcoholic! Where had Matthew come up with that? That was no coincidence. Alex's face burned, but Matthew stared straight ahead at the teacher.

Stunned, Alex glanced at the half-asleep students around her. No one seemed to know that that scuz Matthew was talking about *her.* How had Matthew found her birth records or known her dad belonged to AA? He was forced to join after being jailed for drunk driving; did Matthew know that, too? How?

With a blinding flash, Alex knew. After she'd insulted Hutch earlier that morning, Matthew must have researched *her* in computer lab! Now he was tormenting her with the information, like a cat toying with a mouse before killing it.

Alex sat with her head bowed the rest of the class, her long hair covering her face. She didn't dare look at Matthew. If he had any doubts about his information, her horrified expression would give her away. The rest of the hour was pure torture.

After school, Alex brooded on the way home. Light snow fell, dusting her shoulders and hair. She was nearly home before she'd formulated a plan. She'd do her *own* Internet search. Two could play that game. She bet Hutch had a criminal record somewhere. She'd reveal Hutch's true character, then make him give her grandparents back their money.

Yes, Alex thought, *I'll expose Hutch and give Matthew a choking taste of his own medicine.* Oh, she'd head back to Texas soon, but she'd leave Matthew something real good to remember her by.

chapter.6

The next day was the big out-of-town swim meet. "Wish us luck." Morgan slammed her locker. "Sure you won't change your mind about coming?"

"Nah, you guys'll do great." *Especially with Miss Perfect taking my spot,* she thought.

Waving, Alex headed toward the computer lab. Alex's grandparents didn't expect her home till seven because of the meet, so she planned to work on her people search till the lab closed. The information she could dig up would depend on the facts she started with. The night before, in casual conversation, she'd learned from Grandma that Hutch's last name was Hutchinson. His first name was either David or Douglas, Grandma thought. That was enough to go on, since Alex knew his exact street address.

Matthew was going to pay for what he'd done to her in health class.

Soon Alex was clicking away through various locator tools. Since she didn't know Hutch's previous jobs, she skipped Internet Yellow Pages and went straight to www.worldpages.com and their People Search.

However, Alex was soon frustrated. She typed in several variations—David Hutchinson, Dave Hutchinson, Doug Hutchinson, Douglas Hutchinson—but nothing at all matched with his current address in Edgewood.

Then she tried the same facts at SuperPages.com. This time she turned up nearly two dozen variations in thirteen different states, but none for Indiana. Alex tried four different search engine people finders, with similar results. She did find a *Davis* Hutchinson in Indiana this time, but not in Edgewood.

"Oh, brother," she muttered. She was getting nowhere. What she really wanted was the dirt on old Hutch, but how could she find it?

Back at "Ask Jeeves," she typed, *"Where do you find criminal records?"* and clicked *Ask!* Fifty sites popped up, but only a few looked promising. She tried cybercop.org, but it turned out to be a place to report gripes, abuse, and suspicious activity on the Net.

"No good," she muttered, hitting the *Back* button. "Wait! There's one."

It was called Holding Cell: a list of suspicious characters.

However, a quick click showed it was a list of "cyber abusers," people on the Net accused of false advertising.

Next she tried Metro Area Criminal Court Records. At last! Alex wiped her sweaty hands on her jeans, leaned closer to the screen and read:

**This search indexes all Felony and Misdemeanor
Courts in the selected area. Search results generally
include the date of arrest or offense, charge,
case number, and all information relevant to the arrest.
This search covers the past seven years.**

Alex grinned, but her smile faded as she read on. The criminal search required a full name, date of birth, and a *forty-dollar fee*!

Slumped back in her chair, Alex stared at the computer till it went to the multicolored screen saver. She was stalled everywhere she turned and—

"Having fun, are we?"

Matthew's voice in her ear jolted her upright. Her knee hit the table, which jarred her computer and brought the screen back up. Alex grabbed the mouse and closed the window.

Matthew leaned over her shoulder. "What nasty thing are you hiding?"

Gathering up her notes, Alex turned, and her voice slashed through the quiet computer lab. "How dare you accuse *me* of doing something nasty? I'm not stupid. I know who you were talking about in health class." She backed away from him. "Considering your own poor excuse for a father, you have a lot of nerve."

She was out the lab door in ten seconds. Outside, she headed uptown to the public library to kill some more time. After an hour leafing through magazines, Alex felt it was safe to go home.

Supper was already over, but Alex sniffed at the oven-fried chicken aroma still in the air. She called "I'm home!" then stuck her head in the refrigerator. Excellent! Three left over pieces. She'd eat two of them and sneak the other one upstairs for Maverick.

Just then Grandma pattered into the kitchen. "How'd your meet go tonight?"

Alex reached into the cupboard for a glass. "My time stunk." Her mournful tone added, *And I really don't want to talk about it.* "Can I take this to my room? I have a ton of homework."

"Sure, honey. Take some paper napkins." Grandma pulled her yellow sweater more tightly around her, reminding Alex of a plump canary. "Now don't work too hard."

"No fear." Alex hoisted her backpack to her shoulder, grabbed the plate of chicken and a glass of milk, and headed upstairs. She nodded at her grandfather when she passed through the living room, but apparently he was asleep in the chair sitting up.

Upstairs, she shredded bits of chicken into Maverick's food dish. Then she gnawed on a chicken leg while connecting to the Internet to check her e-mail. *Surely* there would be some word from her mom today. Two e-mail messages loaded. One was from Grandma, a poem called "Don't Ever."

The other message was from her mom!

Wiping her greasy fingers on her jeans, Alex swallowed her disappointment that the message was short.

Hi, Sweetie!

I've only got a minute before the supervisor breathes down my neck again, but I've missed talking to you. I'm using tomorrow's paycheck to reconnect the phone. If you still have your phone cards, call home this weekend. Your father found a different part-time job two days ago. It's in construction. He doesn't really like it, but I hope he'll stick with it anyway. If he can hold down this job and bring home his paychecks, we can fly you home for spring break! Gotta run—here comes the boss!

Mom

xoxoxoxoxoxoxoxoxoxoxoxoxoxoxoxoxoxoxoxo

Alex leaned back in her chair, chewing thoughtfully. No mention of why her mom hadn't written lately. And her dad had *another* job. She'd lost count of the jobs he'd held over the years. Getting him to bring home his paycheck instead of drinking it away had been the real challenge. She shivered as she recalled the bitter fights when he'd finally come home—if he showed up at all.

She'd definitely call home this weekend, but she wouldn't breathe a word about her escape plan. Her mom might not agree to it, but if she just showed up, she knew her mom would be thrilled. They had this special bond, more than mother and daughter. In fact, Alex mused, she often felt more like the mom than the kid.

Just then there was a knock on the door. "You have company, Alex," her grandmother said, opening the door for Morgan. "I'm sorry the meet didn't go well, dear."

Morgan frowned. "What do you mean? We won tonight, by a big margin."

Grandma blinked. "But I thought Alex said . . . Oh dear, am I all confused again?"

Alex stared at the floor, then finally up at her puzzled grandmother. "No, that's what I said. I was going to tell you soon." She licked her lips. "I quit the team." Except for the hum of the computer and purring of the cat under her chair, the room was silent.

"You're taking some time off?"

"No, I quit for good."

"But Alex, why?" Grandma searched Alex's face, then turned toward Morgan, who looked away. "You're such a good swimmer. Why quit in the middle of the season? You were doing so well."

"I can explain, but not now."

Grandma poked a strand of loose hair back into her bun.

"Hmmm. Well, we'll definitely talk about this later," she finally said. "Good to see you, Morgan."

Alex was silent as her grandmother closed the door. "Sorry 'bout that. It's cool that the team won tonight," she said. "Really." After an awkward pause, she turned back to the computer. Her eyebrows rose. "Looks like I've got more mail." She clicked on the little green arrow, then waited for the message to load. When it popped up on the screen, she read quickly. "Morgan, listen to this! It's from someone named Onyx."

My husband is a police officer. He ran a background check on Hutch. You're right to be worried! He's a felon. Go to the web site listed below and type in HUTCHIN-SON, DONALD and see for yourself. --Onyx

"Oh man, oh man!" Alex said. "We've got him now!" She clicked on the site called Web Net Detective, typed in *Hutchinson, Donald*, waited nearly a minute, then up popped a rap sheet a mile long. "No wonder I couldn't find this in the lab today. Grandma thought his name was Douglas or David."

The list of crimes was impressive, for a felon: breaking and entering, assault with a deadly weapon, a bank theft, stolen cars. It was better—and scarier—than anything Alex had expected. Thank goodness she'd found this before her grandparents turned over their life savings to that phony goody-goody!

And, Alex thought grimly, wait till Matthew realized she

knew all about Hutch. This rap sheet made her own dad look like a choir boy.

"What now?" Morgan leaned over Alex's shoulder to read. "Hutch is dangerous! Thank goodness he got away from us Saturday night."

"How can you say that? We could have caught him red-handed!"

"You'd better tell someone," Morgan warned. "Don't try to handle this guy on your own like you do everything else."

"Look, I know what I'm doing. You're sworn to secrecy, too. This information can't be revealed until just the right time. Understand?"

"I don't like it, but okay." Morgan paused. "Just be careful." Alex hit *Reply*.

Onyx: thanx for the info! Keep me informed if your husband discovers what Hutch is doing in Edgewood. It can't be good!

She hit *Send*, then sat back in satisfaction. Finally some good news.

"Strange name, Onyx," Morgan said. "Isn't that a stone for jewelry? My mom had a necklace with a dark stone, and I think she called it onyx."

"Yeah, I think so." Alex stared at the message, lost in thought. "What if I get more mail from Onyx? I can't call you, not with the phone in the living room right by Grandpa's recliner. Can I forward you messages without Maya getting them?"

"I don't know how. She knows my e-mail password."

Alex snapped her fingers. "Wait a sec. I'll put private messages in code."

"I don't know any codes."

"Yes, you do. You just don't know it." Alex opened a word processing window. "I found this one day when I was playing around. Watch."

Alex typed a sample message:

I've got more info on Hutch, so call me!

"Suppose I wanted to forward you this message. First I highlight it, then click on the *Font* button." It said, "Barmeno," but when Alex clicked it, up popped dozens of choices. "Let's try Graeca II. It looks like Greek." She clicked on Graeca II, and suddenly her sample message read:

"Ἰϵ γοτ μορϵ ινφο ον Ηυτχη, σο χαλλ μϵ!"

"Wow! That's cool," Morgan said, "but how can I read it when it comes like that?"

"No sweat." Alex highlighted the rows of symbols, clicked on the *Font* button again, and selected Barmeno. "Presto," she said, as it changed back to the former message.

"I love it! Maya won't know what the message says, even if she opens my e-mail."

Alex lifted her long hair high on top of her head. "I have a feeling this Onyx lady's going to be a real gold mine." *Yup, I'll nail Hutch,* Alex thought, *then I'm off to Texas for good.* It couldn't happen soon enough to suit her.

chapter.7

Opening her bookmark file, Alex found TodaysGirls.com and clicked it. When it loaded, she skimmed Amber's Thought for the Day.

Matthew 7:2: You will be judged in the same way that you judge others. Remember, girls: If you're shrewd in finding the defects in others, others will do the same to you. Let's just love each other!

"Oh, gag," Alex muttered. "Amber gets so preachy."

Morgan pulled a bench over near the computer. "She's right, though. I hate it when 'pretend friends' cut each other down behind their backs."

Alex clicked on the chat room icon. "But why be a fake like Amber and pretend to love everybody?"

She logged in with her password. Since they'd all just ridden home together from the meet, Alex was surprised to find three names in the chat room already: chicChick, faithful1 and nycbutterfly.

> TX2step: congrats on the BIG win! How did u manage w/o me?
>
> nycbutterfly: we want u bak! Amber almost drowned, swimming w/her face in the H20
>
> faithful1: glub, glub. Maya's right. Kum bak. All is 4given. JLY & we do 2!

Annoyed, Alex ignored the last remark. Like she had anything to be forgiven for! Anyway, they obviously didn't need her on the team. Secretly Alex wished they'd lost without her. She didn't like not being needed at all.

> TX2step: Morgan's here.
>
> nycbutterfly: Morgan, I'll pick u up in fifteen if I stay awake that long. yawn.
>
> faithful1: hey, TX, we still need u guys 4 R variety show.
>
> TX2step: sorry, can't dance or sing.
>
> faithful1: not a problem. u can raise $$$ 4 it, since u have extra time on ur hands now

nycbutterfly: we have jobs lined up 4 u

"What's your sister talking about?" Alex said.

"That list of people from church, the ones willing to pay kids for doing odd jobs."

"No way."

TX2step: can't help u. no car 2 get 2 jobs.

faithful1: u r in luck. 1 guy is right next door 2 u. Hutch wants his kitchen cleaned.

"Yes!" Alex let out a shrill whistle. "Bingo. We can search inside his house if we go clean his kitchen."

TX2step: in that case, we'd b glad 2 help. Morgan & me together.

faithful1: kewl! I'll tell him 2 Xpect u both 2morrow.

nycbutterfly: Yo, Morgan, parents r on war path. I'm picking U up NOW.

TX2step: I will push her out door. she's grabbing my leg and won't let go. She's fixin' 2 take a bite out of it. CUL8R

faithful1: thanx! AIMP

nycbutterfly left the room

"AIMP?" Alex frowned as she exited the chat room.

"Always in my prayers."

"Oh brother." Alex clicked on her mail icon and watched a message load. "Look! Another one from Onyx!"

Alex: my husband is angry that I told you about Hutch. He stresses that it is *dangerous* to accuse him of anything. Leave it to the police to get evidence. You don't want to make him mad. DON'T ENDANGER YOURSELF! --Onyx

"This Onyx is right," Morgan said, straightening up. "If you accuse Hutch of something, he could take it out on us—or your grandparents."

Alex stared at the fish swimming across her screen saver. She'd have to find a way to search his house while they cleaned the kitchen. Maybe she could ask to use the bathroom and look around. *Stay out of it? I don't think so!*

"Alex?"

"What?" She blinked and turned around. "Oh. Right. I'll stay out of it. We're just cleaning for a worthy cause."

Morgan looked at her suspiciously, then glanced out Alex's bedroom window. "Maya's here." She pulled on her coat and zipped it, and Alex followed her to the top of the stairs.

"See you tomorrow," Morgan said, waving.

Deep in thought, Alex headed back to her room. As she passed her grandparents' bedroom, their raised voices startled her.

"I mean it, Emily!" Grandpa's voice thundered as if he were still in the pulpit. "I'm taking you to see Dr. Fleming this week!"

"But Chester, I'm fine. I'm just tired."

"No arguments. Every day you forget something else. You leave the coffee out of the coffeepot. You're getting worse, and you have to face it."

Alex's stomach tied in knots as she hurried to her room. She *hated* shouting. Even if Grandma was getting forgetful, what right did Grandpa have to yell at her?

At 4:30 the next afternoon, Alex and Morgan knocked on Hutch's back door, armed with paper towels, a mop, garbage bags, floor cleaner, oven cleaner, and glass cleaner.

A whole minute passed before Hutch opened the door. "Ah, the angels of mercy have arrived," he said. "Enter at your own risk."

You can drop the Mr. Charm act, Alex thought, following him inside. Alex cringed when she stepped into the filthy kitchen. Her feet stuck to the muddy tile floor. She wrinkled her nose and looked around bleakly. "*How* much are you paying?"

Alex heard Morgan's gasp, but she didn't care. Before she touched one crusty, germ-infested dish, she wanted to know how much money was in it. And no way was she giving this money to Amber, not when she needed it so much worse herself. If cleaning Hutch's gross kitchen wouldn't pay for half her ticket home, then forget it.

"I told Amber I'd pay thirty dollars for you to scrub the floor, do the dishes, and clean the stove and oven. I'll throw in another twenty if you clean out the refrigerator."

Alex raised one eyebrow in Morgan's direction. This guy *with no job* could afford to give them fifty dollars for cleaning?

"We'll do the fridge, too." She shoved aside a greasy frying pan on the counter and lined up her cleaning supplies. "Um, you can feel free to take off. We'll be here forever."

"No problem. I'll work in the other room."

Darn, Alex thought. If he hung around, snooping would be harder. Still, she'd find a way.

"I thought your grandma was silly buying us rubber gloves, but not anymore!" Morgan pulled on a yellow pair. "Where do we start?"

"Here." Alex pulled a black garbage bag from the box. "Before we can clean anything, we have to find it. You can start with the table."

Morgan shook open the garbage bag. Holding each piece of trash by her fingertips, Morgan tossed dirty paper plates and cups, granola bar wrappers, juice boxes, used straws, and junk mail into her bag. "Hey, look." Morgan held up several empty cat food pouches.

"Must be for the strays, but where are they? Maybe he eats them. Or sacrifices them in some horrible pagan ritual—"

"Oh, stop!"

Alex rubbed her throbbing forehead. "Can't he turn down that blasted TV? He's more deaf than Grandpa."

Alex then approached the fridge with her own garbage bag and yanked open the door. What *was* that smell? Pulling on rubber gloves, she poked here and there. Besides stinking, everything seemed awfully *soft*. Squishy onions, slimy green peppers, apples and potatoes that dented easily.

By the time she filled the garbage bag, the fridge was nearly empty. All that remained was a bottle of soy sauce, two cans of Coke, a tub of soft butter, and a bottle of ketchup.

Alex tiptoed over to the dining room doorway. From the living room the national news blared on the TV. If only he'd leave!

An hour later as Alex dried the last plate, Hutch shuffled into the kitchen. "I've got errands to run." He pulled his wallet from a back pocket. "I'll pay you now in case I'm not back when you leave." Hutch turned in a slow circle. "The transformation is already impressive! I haven't seen the bottom of the sink in weeks."

You can't even do dishes, Alex thought. *It's no wonder you can't hold a job.*

Hutch laid two twenties and a ten on the now-spotless kitchen table. "Thanks a million, girls." He pulled on a camouflage jacket that looked like a souvenir of his trash can hunts.

"No need to thank us," Alex said. *Especially not when you find out what I've planned.*

As his old junker roared out of the driveway, Alex quickly bolted the door. If either Matthew or Hutch returned too soon, she wanted some warning. She scooped the loose bills off the table and stuck them in her jeans pocket.

"Come on. There's no time to waste." They hurried to the

hall closet. "Look at this stuff," Alex said, pulling out floor-length overcoats, ski masks, and goggles. "Disguises!"

"It's just winter stuff. Everybody has it." Morgan shook a ski mask in Alex's face. "My own dad owns one of these."

"Yes, but your family goes skiing. I bet Hutch doesn't." She rummaged farther back in the closet, then let out a low whistle. "Would you look at this? Now do you believe me?"

She dragged out a bulky cardboard box. From it she pulled a make up kit, a flat box containing jewelry, several pairs of men's and women's dark glasses, a collapsible cane, a black cape, and a fur hat.

"*Now* are you satisfied?"

Morgan opened the jewelry case. She poked through several long pearl necklaces, two rings with huge sparkling stones, and some rhinestone barrettes. "Maybe all this stuff belonged to his dead wife."

"Oh, come *on!*" Alex snorted. "This guy has enough disguises to be a different person—even a different gender—every day of the week."

Alex dumped the stuff back in the box and shoved it to the rear of the closet. Then she moved into the living room. A padded rocker had a rip in the seat. The couch's cushions had been tossed on the floor. An ancient TV blared a game show re-run. Alex snapped it off. The eerie silence was almost spooky.

Alex scanned the sparse room, and her eye caught something on the windowsill. "Hey, look at these." She picked up two small clay statues that were painted gold. Obviously handmade, they resembled angels, only with four arms and four hands. The top two hands were praying, and the lower hands held a ball. "They look Oriental or something."

Morgan turned one around and around in her hands. "I saw something like this at church once. We studied Eastern religions and the teacher called it an idol."

"Like something you'd worship, you mean?"

"Maybe."

"Did any of those religions you studied include animal sacrifices?"

Morgan's eyes bulged. She nodded slowly. "Alex, let's get out of here."

"In a minute." Alex turned slowly in a circle, studying the room. Then she frowned. "Did you hear that?" Alex dropped to her knees by the cold air register in the floor. Then she heard it again: a thump. She pressed her ear against the metal grate. More odd noises echoed up from the basement.

"Come on." Alex grabbed Morgan's hand and raced to the kitchen. The basement door was locked with a rusty hook. Why would Hutch lock his basement door? What—or who—was he keeping prisoner down there?

Alex unhooked the door and pulled it open. The dark stairway yawned open before them like a black hole. Alex leaned over and flipped the wall switch by the sink. A dim bulb hanging over the stairs emitted a weak light, revealing sagging wooden steps cluttered with boxes, boots, paint cans, and a toolbox.

"Watch your step." Alex held the railing as she picked her way around the clutter. Morgan was right on her heels.

Faint light filtered in through the basement's cracked windows. Wind coming through the cracks blew cobwebs back and forth in a gentle swaying rhythm. The basement consisted of several small cement-block rooms, all empty, until they came to the furnace room. There several wooden crates, nailed shut, were stacked one on top of the other.

"Stolen goods, I bet," Alex said.

From behind her came a faint scratching noise. Morgan grabbed Alex's arm and dug in till her nails left tiny indentations in Alex's skin. "What was that?"

Alex turned. Behind the furnace was a small wooden door, also latched on the outside. It reminded her of the old coal storage room in her grandparents' basement. The scratching became louder and more insistent.

Whoever—or whatever—Hutch was holding captive was determined to get out!

chapter.8

Alex shook off Morgan's hand before her fingernails cut the skin. Her own heart pounded so hard she could barely breathe. The scratching behind the locked door quit, then started up again.

Morgan backed up a step. "What's in there?"

Just then a faint *meow* was heard. Alex clapped a hand over her mouth in relief. "Look!" At the bottom of the door, a tiny yellow paw was pushed out in the gap beneath the door.

"He's got those cats locked up?" Morgan moved quickly to unlatch the door.

The second she did, four quick blurs of color—yellow, black, and gray—streaked out and behind the furnace. Alex knelt on the floor and wiggled her fingers. "Here, kitties. Come here. We won't hurt you."

One by one, three of the cats slowly approached, but the fourth one—a medium-sized calico—hung back. Alex sat cross-legged on the cold cement floor while the three cats encircled her. The gray tomcat rubbed his face on Alex's knee, while the yellow tabby sat down and began washing a front paw. Alex looked up and grinned. "I must smell like Maverick."

Morgan laughed, then reached for the calico. Just before her fingers touched fur, the cat dashed into the other room.

"Stop her! Don't let her get upstairs!" Alex coaxed two of the cats back to their room, but the black one darted behind the furnace. Alex crawled after it, sneezing at the dust she stirred up, and grabbed him around the middle.

Morgan's panicky voice echoed from the next room. "Come here! No! Stop! Not up there!" Footsteps clomped halfway up the stairs, then stomped back down again.

The black cat squirmed and clawed Alex. "Stop screaming, Morgan!" she shouted.

"Then you catch this cat!" she yelled back. "I fell on the stairs and like broke my leg. And I'm bleeding. Are you happy now?"

"Oh good grief." Alex closed the black cat in the locked room with the others.

"Look, you rotten cat," Morgan yelled, "come out here!"

Rolling her eyes, Alex stood and brushed the filth and cobwebs off her jeans. Just then, she heard distinct footsteps directly overhead in the kitchen. *Hutch was back!*

Alex raced to the next room where Morgan was crouched

under a work table. A cat's glowing eyes peered out from beneath the bench.

Above them, heavy footsteps crossed to the open basement door. The door slammed shut. Alex heard the hook slip into place.

The last thing she saw before the basement light blinked out was Morgan's terrified face.

The darkness was thick and bone-chilling. "Alex?" Morgan whispered. Alex could hear her crawling toward her across the cement floor. "Alex?"

"Keep coming. I'm right here," she whispered back.

Heart pounding so hard her ears were ringing, Alex crouched down before her wobbly legs collapsed. *Now what?* They'd been caught snooping, and by a convicted felon! What was he going to do with them? Or *to* them?

Just then Morgan bumped into her. Alex wrapped an arm around her trembling friend. "It's okay," she whispered. "We'll get out of here."

"How? I heard him lock the door. The windows down here are too small to crawl out of, even if we broke them."

"I know." Alex swallowed the lump that rose in her throat. What had she gotten them into? If anything happened to them, it would be all her fault.

Morgan hiccuped. "Let's break a window and scream. Your grandparents will hear us."

Alex groaned inwardly. "They might if they were home.

They went to the grocery store." Anyway, Alex suspected, if they started screaming, Hutch would be downstairs strangling—or shooting—them before anyone heard.

Morgan's hiccuping grew louder. "I think I'm going to hurl."

"No, you're *not*. Now listen to me." Alex forced herself to speak calmly. She'd gotten them into this, and she'd get them out. "I think I heard him leave. We'll force the basement door open. A rusty hook's all that's holding it shut. We can pull it out of the wood."

"What if he's waiting in the kitchen?"

"I don't think he is. If he's smart, he already left. He could hit the interstate and cross into Illinois in an hour." She forced phony confidence into her voice.

"I didn't hear his car leave, though."

"Me either," Alex admitted, "but we have to do something right away. He might be getting a rope to tie us up. Come on." Alex stood and shuffled in the direction of the stairs. Six steps later, her ankle bashed into the bottom stair. "Ow. I found it." She pulled Morgan close. "Now, hold on to the railing. Tight."

Gripping hands, they started up the stairs. Halfway up, Alex ran into a thick net of cobwebs. They clung to her eyelashes, and she sucked in a mouthful. "Ugh," she cried, spitting and sputtering to get rid of them.

At the top of the stairs, they shoved on the latched door, leaning their shoulders hard into the wood. A thin crack of light shone beneath the door, but no sounds came from the kitchen.

"Push harder!" Alex grunted and shoved with all her strength, but it was no good. It didn't budge.

"Now what?" Morgan whispered.

"We'll pound on the door and beg him to let us out. Maybe he didn't realize we were down here when he closed the door." Alex searched frantically for a believable explanation. "I'll say we needed something to unclog the sink, so we looked in the basement."

"You think he'll believe that?"

Not if he has the brains God gave a horny toad, Alex thought. Aloud she said, "Why wouldn't he? It makes perfect sense." She took a deep breath. "Here goes."

She knocked lightly at first. When there was no response, she pounded hard. "Hutch! Hutch? Open the door! We accidentally got locked in the basement!"

Then she heard them: footsteps crossing the kitchen. Alex was half relieved and half terrified. "Get ready," she whispered.

Slowly the hook was lifted, and the door swung open. Temporarily blinded by the light, Alex and Morgan stumbled into the kitchen.

"Look what the cat dragged in," Matthew drawled. "Howdy, *y'all.*" He burst out laughing.

Matthew? Alex couldn't believe it! She itched to smack him in his smart mouth. "Thanks for locking us in the basement. We were looking for drain cleaner."

Matthew glanced at the cleaners lined up by the sink. "Yeah, right." He pushed back his greasy hair and rubbed his bleary eyes. "I thought someone was being murdered downstairs. What a rude awakening from my beauty nap."

"Your nap?" Alex blinked. He'd been upstairs all this time? Thank goodness Matthew didn't wake up when they were searching through the closets!

Ignoring Matthew until he shuffled out of the room, Alex sprayed the inside of the fridge with cleaner that smelled like bleach. In her rubber gloves, she scoured until there was nothing left but the rusty spots. By then, Morgan had mopped the floor till it was actually green and white again.

"Let's go." Flexing her aching shoulder, Alex gathered up the cleaning bottles and mop. "Can you come over?"

"Mom said to come straight home."

"Okay, see you tomorrow." Alex crossed the adjoining snowy yards to her back door. Her grandparents' car was still gone, and she was glad. She wanted to e-mail Onyx right away about those disguises.

But upstairs in her room, she forgot about that when she checked her e-mail account and found a private message from a guy in the Neighborhood Watch group.

Tonight I saw your neighbor Hutch go into Mickey's Pawn Shop. I looked in the window. He had a CD player and some jewelry and a wad of cash. Pawning stolen goods, you think?--Joe

That's *exactly* what Alex thought! So that was his errand tonight! He probably pawned a few stolen things from those crates whenever he needed cash. Just wait till Morgan saw this message. If she wasn't convinced before, she would be now.

Alex highlighted the message from Joe, then converted it to Graeco II:

Τονιγητ Ι σαω ψουρ νειγηβορ Ηυτχη γο ιντο Μιχκεψ''σ Παων Σηοπ. Ι λοοκεδ ιν τηε ωινδοω. Ηε ηαδ α ΧΔ πλαψερ ανδ σομε´ εωελρψ ανδ α ωαδ οφ χαση. Παωνινγ στολεν γοοδσ, ψου τηινκ̃--´οε

After sending the coded e-mail, Alex logged on to TodaysGirls.com to see who was around. If Morgan was there, she'd tell her to pick up her e-mail like pronto. Only Jamie and Bren were there.

chicChick: r u going 2 the basketball game 2morrow nite?

rembrandt: Have I ever gone 2 a BB game?

chicChick: y not? The boys from Jackson R going 2 B there!

rembrandt: Do I know any boys from Jackson? I have 2 work anyway.

chicChick: r u going, Alex?

Tx2step: Maybe. I'll C.

Actually, she knew she wouldn't. Getting permission to go out on a school night was like a major hassle. Hardly worth it. It was another one of Grandpa's ancient rules, like "family togetherness" on Sundays.

After exiting the chat room, Alex dug in her pocket for a stick of gum and found Hutch's fifty dollars. She smoothed out the wrinkled bills, then reached for the Christmas tin on her closet shelf where she stashed her money. Her arm knocked two brand-new sweaters to the floor, Christmas presents from her grandparents. "We know how cold you must be," they'd said.

Cold? Sure, but she'd frostbite her entire bod before she'd wear those sweaters. The style was for somebody her mom's age. As Alex fingered a tag still on the sweater, a brilliant idea struck her. Of course! She could take back the sweaters, turn them into cash! She wouldn't need the sweaters in Texas anyway.

Alex slowly surveyed her chilly room. What else could she sell in order to buy her ticket sooner? It didn't have to be new. There were pawnshops downtown.

Hmmm . . . There was that soft-side luggage under the bed, and her bedside lamp which she hardly used. The birthstone necklace from Christmas was still in its velvet box. What about her army surplus jacket? It was all her own stuff. She could do what she wanted with it.

Mentally adding it up, Alex headed down to the kitchen for a snack. As she reached the bottom of the stairs, she heard the back door open. Paper sacks crackled as her grandparents carried in groceries.

Oh good! Food! Alex thought. But she halted in the living room when her grandfather said, "It'll be fine, Emily. The doctor will run tests tomorrow and find out what's wrong."

"I'm not worried. Isn't that nice of Hutch to drive us into the city? What a thoughtful man," Grandma said. Paper rattled and cupboard doors opened and closed.

Alex froze. Hutch was driving them into the city the next day? If her grandparents were gone for hours, she could skip school and drag her belongings down to the pawnshop. If Hutch were in the city with them, he wouldn't be home to spy on her.

Just then Grandpa McGee shuffled wearily into the living room. He collapsed in his recliner and stared blankly at the dark TV screen.

"Are you okay?"

Grandpa blinked, then nodded. "I didn't see you." He gripped the chair arms, looking dry and stiff as a well-preserved mummy.

"Um, I heard you talking about seeing the doctor tomorrow."

Grandpa listened for sounds from the kitchen. When he finally spoke, his voice was so low that Alex had to crouch near his chair to hear. "I already know what's wrong with your grandma."

"You do?"

He removed the rimless glasses that slid down his nose and rubbed his eyes. "As a pastor, I visited many nursing homes. I've seen dozens of cases like this."

"What do you mean?"

"Alzheimer's disease."

"Alzheimer's?" Alex's throat almost closed up. Even she'd heard of that on TV shows. Old people gradually forgot who they were. They didn't recognize family members, they couldn't be left alone, and then they died. "You honestly think Grandma has Alzheimer's?"

He nodded, then blinked rapidly as his eyes filled. "Don't say it in front of Grandma. She doesn't know yet. Tomorrow the doctor will help her—and me—face the truth."

At that, he dropped his head into his gnarled hands. Alex stared down on the top of his head. Long strands of gray hair, carefully combed, barely covered a pink bald spot the size of a silver dollar. Alex stood awkwardly, then reached out to pat his shoulder, but pulled her hand back before touching him. She didn't know what to do—or say.

Grandma McGee couldn't be that sick, could she? But Grandpa was so sure.

Turning, Alex stumbled from the room and climbed upstairs.

chapter.9

Thursday morning Alex got ready for school as usual, picking the least dirty jeans and corduroy shirt from the pile on the floor of her closet. She left at her regular time, then hung out in McDonald's until time for Hutch to drive her grandparents to the doctor. Finally, at nine-thirty Alex went home and slipped inside, using her spare key.

In less than five minutes she'd grabbed her duffel bag, plus the cash she'd saved, and was back on the sidewalk. She had the fifty dollars from Hutch, thirty from her lunch money, plus fifteen dollars Christmas money she'd saved.

She'd jotted down the address of the pawnshop from the phone book, and it was only five blocks from the bus station. After selling her stuff, she'd go straight to the bus station and buy her one-way ticket to freedom. All she needed was thirty more dollars, and she figured her stuff was worth fifty at least.

She found Mickey's Pawn Shop without any trouble. "Buy, Sell & Trade! Money to Lend!" read the blinking sign outside. It wasn't what Alex expected. On TV rich ladies took jewels and fur coats to pawnshops that looked like department stores. Mickey's Pawn Shop, by contrast, had filthy windows covered with bars.

Alex stepped inside the dimly lit building, holding her nose against the musty smell. A bell above the door jangled. A man with heavy bags under his eyes stepped through a flowered curtain hung on a rod across a doorway.

"Yeah?" he asked, wiping a hand across his mouth.

Alex stared at his mustache. Bits of scrambled eggs speckled it. "Um, I . . ." She hefted her bag up onto the smudged glass counter. "I have stuff to sell."

The proprietor wiggled a mustache that resembled dirty toothbrush bristles. Without a word, he rummaged through Alex's belongings. "Don't want the lamp." He pointed to a shelf with four similar lamps. "I'll give you thirty for the rest of it."

"Thirty? That's a ripoff!" Alex adjusted the sweaters to show the price tags. "It's new, some of it. I want fifty at least."

The man shrugged, picked a piece of egg out of his mustache and ate it, then headed back toward the curtained doorway.

"Wait!" Alex held up her duffel bag. "Did you count this heavy bag? It goes with the stuff."

The man hiked up his baggy pants and tucked in his plaid flannel shirt. "Thirty-five then. That's it."

"I'll take it." Alex looked at the lamp. She wasn't carrying that thing to the bus station and back home. "I'll throw in the lamp for free."

The man studied the tags still attached to the sweaters. "You sure this stuff belongs to you?"

"Well what do you think?" Alex snapped. "If I wanted to shoplift, I'd steal something better than old lady sweaters."

Without response, he opened the cash register and counted out thirty-five dollars. As soon as Alex had it in her hand, she was out the door.

Fifteen minutes later Alex arrived at the bus terminal, purchased her one-way ticket for Saturday night, then was out the door again, the ticket tucked carefully in the pages of her health book. She was giddy thinking about how soon she'd see her mom.

Alex still had all afternoon to kill so she could return home at her regular time, so she headed to the mall. By the time she returned to her grandparents' four hours later, the excitement of buying her bus ticket had been replaced by very real fear for her grandparents. What if Grandpa was right about Grandma's illness? What if Alex couldn't trap Hutch before Saturday? What if he was being nice to her grandparents in order to steal their life savings? They were so gullible! Gritting her teeth, Alex was determined to nail Hutch very soon.

When she stepped into the warm kitchen, she was met by

the mouth-watering aroma of homemade cinnamon rolls. Grandma was frosting them, humming some song Alex recognized from church.

"Hi!" Alex reached for a roll and stuffed half of it in her mouth, smearing frosting down her chin. "So, how was your appointment?"

Grandma beamed. "After some blood tests, the doctor said I just need some vitamins."

Alex swallowed hard. "Vitamins? For being forgetful?" That didn't sound right.

Alex ate her second roll more slowly, then licked the cinnamon off her fingers. "I'm glad it was something simple."

Heading up to her room, she met her grandfather coming down the stairs. "I just talked to Grandma," she said. "I'm glad the doctor had good news."

Grandpa McGee stared through her as if she were a pane of glass.

"Grandpa?"

He gripped the railing and cleared his throat. "The doctor wants her to be happy, but he knows the truth as well as I do. I could tell by the look on his face."

"He lied to her?"

"Yes, and for your grandmother's sake, we'll play along. Otherwise she'll spend what time she has left at home worrying about us."

Alex gulped and turned away. She had a sinking feeling her

grandfather was right. Alzheimer's was common in old age. If memory loss was cured with something as simple as vitamins, nobody'd have that problem. Her heart heavy, she went on up the stairs.

In her room a moment later Alex checked TodaysGirls.com and found nycbutterfly, jellybean, and faithful1 in the chat room. Alex scanned their messages. They were discussing something Coach had said after the last meet.

With a sharp pang Alex realized how much she missed being part of the relay team. Actually, it was the only part of school she'd liked.

faithful1: Hey, Alex! WB! How's it going?

TX2step: K

jellybean: R U sick? Missed U 2day.

TX2step: doing better.

nycbutterfly: Actually I feel sick 2 my stomach 2, cuz I have 2 give my language speech tomorrow, & I am so not ready.

chicChick enters the room

chicChick: News flash! I was @ the mall. When did Janna & Nathan get so friendly? I thought he was w/Leah!

faithful1: U would think she'd have enough sense not 2 go out w/him.

chicChick: They did look kinda cute 2gether, but poor Leah!

Alex rubbed her eyes, the lack of sleep catching up with her. She could care less who Bren saw at the mall. Big deal.

TX2step: Gotta go lay down. CU 2morrow.
faithful1: AIMP

Alex clicked *Exit,* surprised that this time it didn't annoy her to know she'd be in Amber's prayers. Actually, she was probably going to need them.

Next Alex e-mailed Onyx about the disguises hidden in Hutch's house, then asked her to pass along the information to her husband. She clicked *Send,* then closed her browser.

Exhausted by all the walking she'd done that day, Alex flopped down on her bed. She was barely aware, before falling asleep, of Maverick curling up in a ball against her stomach. Alex drifted off to the rhythm of gentle purring.

After supper Thursday night, Alex's bedroom was an oven from leaving the heater cranked up to high. She propped her window several inches, then sorted through her clothes. Shaking out her shirts, she watched cat hair fly up and float down around her. Ugh. She'd stuff as many of her clothes as she could in her school bag, then send for the rest later.

She was choosing what tapes to take along for the bus ride when she heard a loud knock on their back door below. Curious,

Alex knelt by her window and listened. A moment later her grandfather's voice drifted upward.

"Hello! Twice in one day. Come in, come in."

"Sorry, I can't stay. Could we talk a minute?"

Alex perked up at the sound of Hutch's scratchy voice. What did he want?

"Is anything wrong?" her grandfather asked.

"I don't like to spread tales, but being the parent of a teenager, I'd want to know."

"Know what?"

"I'm sorry, Chet, but Matthew says Alex is skipping school, including today."

"Oh, no." There was a long pause. "I've been concerned since she quit the swim team. If I hadn't been so worried about Emily . . . No, that's no excuse. I should have gotten to the bottom of Alex's attitude lately."

At that, Alex seethed. What was wrong with her attitude? Considering all the people attacking her lately, she'd been down-right Miss Congeniality. That creep Matthew! He wasn't in school every day either! She leaned close to the screen to catch Hutch's next words.

"Matthew said she and her friend were acting strange when cleaning my kitchen last night. Um, did she mention anything to you?"

Aha! Alex thought. The real reason he was here! Hutch suspected Alex was on to him, and he was pumping her grandfather to find out what she knew!

"No, she didn't say anything, at least not to me," her grandfather said.

"Well, I just thought you'd want to know about school."

"Yes, thank you."

After she heard the kitchen door close and she watched Hutch go home, Alex closed her window and pulled the shade. What exactly had Matthew said about her and Morgan? Did Hutch suspect how much they really knew? If so, *what did he plan to do about it?*

Alex hid in her room all evening, expecting a visitor, but no one came to lecture her about skipping school. Curled up in bed that night, with Maverick purring in her ear, Alex couldn't shake her guilty feelings. Why did buying that bus ticket make her feel like a juvenile delinquent running away from home? She was running *to* home!

Friday morning, on her way out the kitchen door, her grandfather stopped her. "One moment, Alexandra."

Alex stopped, staring at the linoleum floor. *Here it comes,* she thought.

But all he said was, "It's important that you attend school every day." She glanced up when he didn't say anything else. "Do we understand each other?" he asked.

Alex nodded.

That day after school Morgan followed Alex home. Up in Alex's room, they logged on to collect Alex's e-mail. "Look! Another one."

Urgent! This is private, so keep it quiet, but something is brewing. Several cars in town were broken into last night--stereo equipment and cell phones stolen. Sounded like Hutch's rap sheet. Police need hard evidence. Keep your eyes open. --Onyx

Morgan read the message over Alex's shoulder. "Don't even *think* about investigating on your own." Morgan swiveled Alex's chair around until they were face to face. "I mean it. I won't keep quiet if you go back into his house. It's too dangerous."

"Get a grip!" Alex drummed her fingers on the desk. "This needs to be a neighborhood alert." She typed quickly:

Friends: Guard your cars! Stereo equipment and cell phones are being stolen. Report any suspicious persons seen around parked cars. Remember: Hutch's rap sheet included auto theft. Sounds like our man. PLEASE FORWARD.

"There." Alex clicked the *Send* button, then turned around. "Now all we have to do is—" She stopped abruptly when Morgan knocked her books off the bed. The bus ticket fell from Alex's health book and fluttered to the floor.

"What's this?" Morgan turned it sideways and squinted to read. "Burnet, Texas? You're visiting your parents? Rock!"

"Uh, yeah." Alex reached out to take the ticket. "I was going to tell you."

Morgan frowned, lifting the ticket out of Alex's reach. "Wait a minute. This is a one-way ticket to Texas. For tomorrow night! What are you thinking?"

Alex chewed her upper lip. "I planned to write . . ."

"You're running away! Aren't you?" Morgan waved the ticket in her face. "Your poor grandparents have no idea, do they?" She started for the door.

Alex jumped up and blocked the exit. "No! Please don't tell them."

"How can you do this? Why didn't you tell me? You're my best friend!" Morgan's eyes filled with tears, and she angrily brushed them away.

"You don't understand."

Morgan threw the bus ticket on the floor and grabbed her coat and books. "You're right. I don't understand *you*. Not at all. And I'm not sure I want to anymore." With that, she left, slamming the bedroom door behind her.

Alex heard Morgan's footsteps pounding down the stairs. Squatting, she picked up her bus ticket and stared till the print blurred. She hadn't felt so alone in a very long time.

chapter.10

After a restless night, Alex was up before dawn Saturday morning. As quietly as she could, she packed what she needed for her trip. An extra set of clothes, a paperback and tapes for the twenty-hour ride, her leftover cash for food, and a few pictures taken at swim meets went into the bag.

For one last time, she logged on to TodaysGirls.com. Jamie's Artist's Corner showed a cartoon caricature of Coach Short, in the pool wearing water wings. Alex laughed out loud.

Then she read Amber's new Thought for the Day for Saturday.

If you think you can judge others, then you are wrong . . . . when you judge them you are really judging yourself guilty. Romans 2:1

No kidding, Alex thought. She felt judged by Morgan, her grandfather, even Coach. None of them knew how she really felt—or why she was desperate to get home. Alex was glad *she* was open-minded, though. No one could accuse her of judging unfairly. All she wanted was to live and let live—and be left alone.

She checked her e-mail and watched one message load. It was a group message from Grandma. Corny as her poems were, Alex hoped Grandma would keep her on her list after she went home. She opened this message and read:

On the Wings of Prayer

Just close your eyes and open your heart,
And feel your worries and cares depart.
Just yield yourself to the Father above,
And let him hold you secure in His love.
For life on earth grows more involved,
With endless problems that can't be solved.
God only asks us to do our best,
Then He will take over and finish the rest . . .
So when you are tired, discouraged, and blue,
There is always one door that is open to you:
And that is the door to the house of prayer—
You'll find God waiting to meet you there.

Alex sniffled, then headed to the bathroom for a tissue. She nearly collided with her grandfather as he emerged from his bedroom. Alex looked once, then again. Grandpa McGee looked odd, and his skin was downright gray.

"You okay?" she asked.

He rubbed his hands together. The rasping of dry skin on dry skin sounded like sandpaper. "Here I am, a man of faith, and I can't seem to deal with life's one true certainty." He stared as if he were viewing a spot in the future only he could see. "It's just that when it happens to you . . ."

"You mean Grandma?" Alex said. "But she seems better."

"Wishful thinking." He seemed to shrink inside his blue cardigan sweater. "I know it's Alzheimer's. No vitamin deficiency could cause dementia. That's just a doctor's white lie to make us feel better. For a while anyway."

Alex cocked her head to one side. If only she could do something to help before she left. "Want me to try to find out?"

Grandpa blinked. "How?"

"With the computer, on the Internet."

Grandpa's eyebrows drew together in one unruly line. "There's no help on that evil machine." He started down the hall, one foot slightly dragging.

"I know it's hard to imagine," Alex snapped, "but you could be wrong. You have no clue what I do on the Internet."

What did her grandfather think, for Pete's sake? That she was checking out porn sites or something? Alex gritted her teeth. She wasn't stupid. She knew some weirdos hung out online, pretending to be a friend your age while they stalked you. She'd seen TV shows about it. That was half the reason they had their own chat room. But an evil machine? Oh, come on!

Grandpa stopped, straightened, then slowly turned back to face her. Alex watched as waves of anger, fear, and hope passed over his face. She waited. Hope finally won out. "Do you really think you could find out something?"

"I could try." Alex reached a hand out toward him. "Come on. I'll see what I can do."

In her room, Alex pulled the vanity bench close so they could both sit down. She wiggled the mouse, bringing the TodaysGirls.com page back into view. "This is my friends' Web site," she explained. "You know, where I chat."

"Oh?" Raising his nose in the air, he peered through the bottom half of his bifocals, then pointed to the Thought for the Day at the top of the screen. "What's that?"

"That's Amber Thomas's area. She goes to your church." In her bookmark file, Alex found her favorite search engine, Ask Jeeves. "What did you call Grandma's problem?"

"Dementia."

"Can you spell it?" As he spelled, Alex typed in her question: "What is dementia?" Then she clicked the red *Ask!* button and waited thirty seconds. "Okay, here's our choices," she said, scrolling down the screen. "This looks like a possibility." Alex clicked on Infoseek's Patient Education Forum on Dementia, then waited. It took another thirty seconds to fully load the Question and Answer page. "Here we go," she said.

She read aloud that dementia was a condition of "declining mental abilities," that people with dementia would have trouble keeping a checkbook, driving a car safely, or planning a meal. They could change in personality, becoming aggressive or depressed. "Aging alone," the article said, "does not cause dementia."

Hmm . . . Not a lot of help there, she thought.

Then Grandpa McGee jerked as if he'd gotten a violent shock. He made a choking sound in his throat and pointed further down the screen. In a wavering voice, he read, "'Alzheimer's disease is the most common type of dementia.' See? The doctor's lying to us!"

"Wait, let's read it all." Alex scrolled down, scanning question after question. Then she spotted it. "Look! Read this," she said, pointing. "'There are many causes of dementia, including strokes, *low vitamin B-12 levels*, thyroid conditions, certain medications, and other infections.'"

Beside her, Alex's grandfather froze. Alex could see the blinking cursor reflected in his glasses. His lips moved silently, as he read and reread that section. "It *does* say her condition could be caused by low vitamin levels. The doctor wasn't lying!"

"Guess not." Alex closed the medical page and returned to her Web site.

Grandpa McGee removed his glasses, rubbed his eyes, then replaced his bifocals and stared at the screen. "If you think you can judge others, then you are wrong," he read aloud. He lowered his chin to his chest and shook his head slowly. "I can see now that I've been very guilty of judging you." He looked at Alex. "I was wrong about you being on the Internet. There *are* some good things here."

"I'm glad if I helped."

He smiled suddenly, and he looked fifteen years younger. "It's funny. I was the minister, but Emily was always better at loving people instead of judging them." He scratched his forehead. "Emily could love the most unlovable people, including me at times. 'Love thy neighbor' wasn't just something she heard in church. She practiced it."

Alex thought of Hutch. *Grandma loving* that *neighbor was a big mistake.* But she bit her tongue. Without concrete evidence, Grandpa would never believe her.

Grandpa stood then, patted Alex's shoulder, and left her room. Alex noted with an unexpected rush of love that he held his shoulders back and head up.

Maverick bounded up into her lap, turned in a complete circle, then coughed and coughed, spitting out a hair ball in her lap. "Oh, guck!" Alex grabbed a tissue and scooped the soggy wad off her lap and threw it in the wastebasket. "Now go away," she said, sitting back down.

Absent-mindedly Alex stared at her screen. There was one more e-mail she needed to send before leaving town.

Since she hadn't been able to expose Hutch yet, she would pass along everything she knew about him to the Neighborhood Watch group. She had to do everything possible to protect her too trusting grandparents.

Before she could start typing, though, the green arrow popped up.

Confidential! The police are closing in on Hutch. My husband warns you again to stay clear! Police have set a trap, and expect to nail him tonight. It will be over soon. --Onyx.

Alex let out a low whistle. Finally! Sounded like Hutch had slipped. She bet he got overconfident, thinking he'd fooled everyone with going to church and taking old people to their doctors. Well, apparently the con was over. Hopefully, before she left town that night, she'd know for sure that her grandparents were safe.

Alex wanted to call Morgan with the news, but from the way she'd slammed out of her room the night before, Alex knew their friendship was over. It hurt worse than she expected. Morgan was the sweetest friend she'd ever had. She'd helped Alex make friends and get on the swim team when she moved to Edgewood.

"Well, I can forward Onyx's message to her. Then she'll know it's almost over," Alex muttered, "and that helping me wasn't wasted."

She highlighted her message and changed it to the funny-looking Greek "code." Then she pasted it into an e-mail addressed to Morgan and pressed *Send*. "Done," she said.

She spent the next two hours cleaning her room, dusting her furniture, and changing the sheets on her bed. She might even write a nice letter for her grandparents. Now that it was time to leave, she found she didn't resent her grandfather nearly as much. This morning they seemed to have reached an understanding.

"You're working hard this morning." Grandma appeared in her doorway, holding a plate of brownies. "Hungry? They're warm from the oven."

"Starved!" Alex dropped the pillowcase she was struggling with and reached for the plate.

"I'm making Swedish meatballs next, for the potluck to-night. Are you coming?"

"I didn't know about any church supper." Alex's mind raced. She could hardly believe her good luck. With her grandparents at church, it'd be a cinch to sneak out to the bus station on time. "I already made plans for tonight," she said.

"I supposed as much. Now don't work too hard." Grandma pulled the door shut behind her to keep the heat in the room.

Alex perched on the edge of her half-made bed and polished off all three brownies. She gave the last bits to Maverick, who politely truned her head away.

She glanced around her room, then out the window to Hutch's house next door. It blew her mind to realize how much had happened in a week. Just last Saturday night Morgan had stayed over, and they'd tracked Hutch on that wild-goose chase at midnight—

Wait a minute! Alex suddenly recalled how they'd lost Hutch down by that huge estate surrounded by the brick wall. What if the police had followed him there, too? It was entirely possible. *Was the important showdown with Hutch taking place there tonight?*

While her grandparents were at the potluck, she'd have time to kill before her bus left. She'd check out that old estate! Alex would give her right arm to see him caught!

By the time her grandparents left for the church supper, Alex was too hyper to sit down. Seeing how happy her grandparents were, she hated knowing that when they returned that night, they'd find her gone. Even though she'd leave a detailed note about her bus schedule, she knew they'd worry anyway.

When her grandmother gave her a hug before leaving, Alex clung longer than she meant to. Grandma stood back from her and smiled. "My, that was nice." She peered closely at Alex. "Are you all right, honey?"

"Sure! I—I just love you," she stammered.

"We love you, too." Grandma laid a gentle hand against her cheek. "Have a wonderful evening, and we'll see you about nine."

"Okay." Alex waved, knowing that by nine o'clock she'd already be on the Greyhound bus, heading for the sunny South.

After they left, Alex double-checked her backpack, putting

the bus ticket right on top. Then she grabbed her winter jacket. She still had two hours before leaving for the bus station. Plenty of time to play her hunch: Alex's gut instincts told her that fancy estate was the site of the planned showdown. She didn't intend to miss it.

Outside, she half walked, half jogged down the sidewalk. It was dark already, but that suited Alex just fine. At least this time, she wasn't wearing kitten pajamas! Her stomach did major flip-flops, but whether it was from tracking Hutch or leaving town that night, she didn't know. She pulled her wool scarf up around her ears to block the wind.

For two blocks she stayed on the north side of the street. As she continued down the third block, passing in and out of dark shadows, Alex gradually became aware of a sound that followed steadily behind her, but never quite caught up.

Turning, she was startled to see a dark car cruising close to the curb. *Oh, man,* Alex thought with a sinking feeling, *is that Hutch's car?* Had he figured out what she knew? Was he waiting to run her over, to kill her?

Hands jammed in her pockets, Alex searched for the nearest house with lights on. The house beside her was dark, and next to it was a vacant lot.

Suddenly the car sped up and passed her, then abruptly pulled to the curb. Alex stifled a scream as the passenger door flew open and a dark figure jumped out.

chapter.11

Alex froze for a split second, then pivoted to race across the vacant lot.

"Alex! Wait!"

Alex halted, then turned and peered into the shadows. "Morgan? Is that you?"

Alex didn't recognize the car, but it was definitely Morgan who stepped out of the shadows. A voice from inside the car called "See you guys later!" as it pulled away.

"Was that Maya?" Alex tried to sound cool, but her heart still pounded like a jackhammer.

"Yeah, they're doing their talent show at some shelter tonight." Morgan shuffled her feet back and forth on the sidewalk, as if to warm them. "She was dropping me off at your house, but I saw you walking this way so we turned around to catch you." She laughed. "At least I *thought* it was you. Your jacket hangs to your knees, so it's hard to tell."

Alex cocked her head to one side. "You were coming to see me? Why? You were spittin' nails when you left last night."

"Sorry. I shouldn't have blown up like that. I never even asked you what your reasons for leaving were."

An unexpected lump rose in Alex's throat. "Not a problem."

"Since you're still here, does that mean you changed your mind?"

"No. The bus doesn't leave for two hours. Thanks for not telling my grandparents."

"You're sure this is the right thing for you?"

Alex clenched her fists inside her roomy jacket pockets. "I have to go." She lifted her chin and looked her friend in the eye. "I'm worried about my mom. I hardly hear from her anymore. Something's wrong. There's no one to take care of her now that I live up here."

"Why does she need taking care of?"

"You wouldn't understand."

"Try me."

Alex hunched her shoulders as if closing in on herself. Her voice was barely above a whisper. "Dad drinks sometimes. Then he yells and throws things. Mom's never gotten *really* hurt, but she gets in the way sometimes." Her voice cracked. "What if she got hurt again, only I wasn't around to help her? Even worse, what if I was having fun up here when it happened? I'd never forgive myself."

Morgan was quiet for a long moment. "I'm sorry. I didn't know."

Alex wiggled her eyebrows at Morgan. "Don't worry. I should've told you awhile back."

Morgan laughed. "What are you doing out here anyway?"

"My grandparents are at a church potluck, so I'm killing some time."

"You mean looking for Hutch, don't you?" At Alex's surprised expression, Morgan added, "I got your coded e-mail about some showdown tonight."

"I forgot I sent that." Alex pointed to the brick wall along the sidewalk a block away. "I have a hunch it's happening there."

"That's where we lost him last weekend, isn't it?"

"Yup, but I don't expect you to come with me this time."

"I can't let you go alone!" Morgan hooked her arm through Alex's.

"Thanks." Wordlessly, they hurried down the block and across the street. The two wrought-iron gates were locked, and at first Alex couldn't see a way to climb the brick wall. Then she noticed a bench at a bus stop, half a block away. "Let's use that to stand on." But when they tried to drag the bench over to the wall, they found it bolted to the concrete.

"How about this?" With her foot, Morgan nudged a round

redwood garbage container. It was also bolted to the ground, but the empty metal trash can inside lifted out.

"Brilliant." Alex helped Morgan lift it out, drag it over to the wall, and turn it upside down. "I'll go first. You stand guard."

Alex crawled up on the can, hoisted one leg over the brick wall, then flung her other leg up and over. She dropped six feet to the ground inside, sinking into ankle-deep snow. *Ugh. Just what I needed,* she thought as she dug the snow out of her shoes.

Morgan joined her just seconds later. Alex scanned the deserted grounds and graveled parking area. Dozens of bushes and weird statues provided multiple hiding places.

"Looks like Mr. and Mrs. Filthy Rich are having a party," Morgan said, pointing to the parking lot that was two-thirds full.

"Great place for someone to break into cars." Alex studied the sprawling brick structure, three full stories high. "Reminds me of those mansions they convert into funeral homes." Alex peered into the shadows. "If the police are staked out waiting for Hutch, they're hiding here somewhere, so watch it."

Together they headed across the wide expanse of lawn toward the three-story brick building. As they approached the ground-floor windows, a high-pitched scream, followed by another softer wail, filled the crisp night air. Morgan grabbed Alex's arm in a death grip.

"Come on." Crouching, Alex dragged Morgan to the bank of windows. One was open several inches. Just then another horror-filled scream split the air. Alex slowly rose high enough to peek inside. The room was empty, but the sight before her took her breath away. "Morgan, get up here and look."

Morgan inched up and peered inside. "What the heck—?"

In the brightly lit room was a row of iron beds with side rails, like something from a hospital. Attached to the side rails were long straps. Alex couldn't believe her eyes. "Those screams," she whispered. "People are tied down in there and tortured!"

They ran around the corner to what looked like a service entrance, where people made deliveries. Alex grabbed the door and yanked it open. They rushed inside, slipping and sliding in their wet shoes on the shiny tile floor.

"Man, it stinks in here." Alex stomped the snow off her shoes, wrinkling her nose at the disinfectant smell. "What is this, servants' quarters?" She tested the doors along the hallway, searching for a phone, but they were all locked.

"Listen." Morgan put a finger to her lips. "What's that?"

Alex's eyes opened wide. The low organ music was very melodramatic. "Some weird party? Or maybe they're showing old horror movies. Come on."

At the end of the hall, the music grew louder, punctuated with laughter. Alex hated to crash this party, but there was no choice. From the sounds of the screams they'd heard just minutes ago, someone was in terrible trouble! At the carved double doors in the central hallway, Alex grabbed the brass handles to yank them open.

Inside, a ballroom was half full of people watching a performance on a makeshift stage. A cardboard locomotive was ready to run over a screaming blonde tied to fake railroad tracks. A black-caped villain loomed over her, then yanked a huge necklace from the heroine's neck.

"Alex, wait," Morgan said.

Alex ignored her and lurched breathlessly up the aisle toward the stage, vaguely aware that these party guests were strange. Some were in bathrobes, some in wheelchairs, almost like a hospital . . .

And then she saw it.

The skit was over, the audience applauded, and the heroine was untied from the tracks. When she stood and curtsied, Alex found herself staring into Amber's eyes. The villain's droopy fake mustache was peeled off to reveal Coach Short! Two people—Maya and Jamie—stepped out from behind the cardboard locomotive and took a bow. So this was their talent show!

Alex scanned the room as the lights came up. All the guests were men, some dressed in regular clothes, some in robes. At least a dozen cats were scattered throughout the room—perching in windows, lying in laps, or napping on the floor.

Then the music stopped. Out from behind the makeshift stage curtain stepped her neighbor, the felon: Hutch.

By then Morgan had joined her. "What's going on?" she whispered.

"I don't know, but we've stumbled into some kind of hospital. A veterans' hospital, I'd guess, since they're all old men."

Just then Maya and Jamie spotted them and waved. "Look who came to help after all!" Amber called. "Come up here!"

Alex shook her head violently. She wouldn't get up there if they paid her.

But as details started to register, she recognized the "disguises" from Hutch's closet. Amber wore the jewels, and Coach had the long cape. The girls pushing the locomotive were dressed in black, with ski masks and gloves to blend into the black curtain. Hutch held the source of the melodramatic music, the portable CD player from Mickey's Pawn Shop.

Morgan nudged her. "Look over there."

Alex turned sideways. Decorating one wall was a huge poster board sign done in pink and orange neon. "PETS FOR VETS! Need a companion? Sign up here!" it said. *So that's what Hutch did with the cats he took in.* Shame and embarrassment washed over Alex in waves.

Next to the pet sign, two dented garbage cans overflowed with cans. "PITCH IN! SAVE THOSE CANS! RECYCLE HERE!" the sign above said. Alex wished she could sink through the floor. So *that's* why Hutch searched everyone's trash. He wasn't stashing drugs; he was collecting cans to make money for the vets' home.

And this old mansion hadn't been converted into a funeral home. It was a VA hospital.

"Let's sit down." Morgan pulled on her arm. "Everyone's staring at us."

"Okay." They slipped into two vacant metal folding chairs, and Alex nodded at the patient next to her in a wheelchair. "Hello," she said, wishing she was anywhere but there.

"I'm an artist." The man with the gray ponytail leaned over the side of his wheelchair. "A sculptor." He held out a small clay statue with four arms. Two hands prayed and two held a gold ball, *just like the statues she'd seen in Hutch's living room.* "Do you like my Goddess of Mercy? It's from Vietnam. We have to remember the dead. If I can just do this one thing, then somehow the war will be all right." Suddenly he was shaking and crying, unable to go on.

Embarrassed and horrified, Alex wanted to run, but no one around them acted like anything out of the ordinary was happening. Was this guy having a flashback? She'd heard about those with the Vietnam vets.

Then, with sudden insight, she realized what she and Morgan had seen down the hall. The hospital beds equipped with straps were to hold down out-of-control patients, maybe like this sculptor, who had horrible flashbacks. Cringing, she reached over to pat the man's shaking hand.

He grabbed Alex's hand and held on. All his knuckles were covered with Band-Aids. "I don't know how to explain it," he wailed. "If I can make one perfect sculpture, then maybe it will never happen again."

"I hope so. I'm sure you're right." Slowly Alex loosened her fingers from his grasp. "Would you maybe like a cat?" she finally asked, but he didn't seem to hear.

Up front, Hutch raised his hands and asked for quiet. "Thank you for your applause! We love having young people here, don't we?" His smile slowly faded. "I'm sorry to announce, however, that this was our last show. Because of some rumors, my funds were cut off." He rubbed the back of his neck. "I've been asked to discontinue my work here."

"No! No! No!" echoed cries from all over the room.

Alex stared at Morgan in horror. "Oh, man, what have I done?"

Hutch was only raising money and doing volunteer work with vets! He wasn't some con man stealing from old people. Because of her, those rumors about his rap sheet had circulated. But—but—they weren't rumors! They were true! Donald Hutchinson *was* a felon. And, according to Onyx, the police in town knew all about it.

What was going on?

Alex jumped up and stumbled over Morgan's feet to reach the aisle. She had to get out. How could she have misjudged Hutch that badly? Where had she gone wrong? Was that rap sheet on the Internet just a phony?

As she strode toward the double doors at the back, Alex spotted Matthew right in front of her, leaning back against the wall. He caught her eye and grinned, like he knew why she was desperate to escape.

With a careless movement, he raised his hand and waved. The overhead lights glittered off his black onyx ring.

chapter.12

Alex skidded to a stop at the sight of the ring. Her voice came out like a strangled hiss. "That's onyx, I presume."

"You're sharp." He bowed low with a sweeping gesture. "Let me introduce myself. I'm Onyx, just your average cop's wife."

Alex stretched to her full height and got within two inches of his face. "You think this is funny, do you? Look what you've done!"

"Look what *I've* done? How would I know you'd take a joke and flap your lips to everyone in town?"

Alex sputtered and spit. "This is your idea of a joke?"

Matthew glanced to where his dad was surrounded by a crowd of men. "I was mad at Dad when I sent you that criminal Web site. I thought I might stir up some trouble for him, especially if you told your grandparents." He laughed then, more like a cackle. "What a stitch watching you and your friend play Nancy Drew."

"Oh yeah? Well, your dad really *is* a criminal. I read his rap sheet!"

"*Tsk-tsk.*" Matthew's eyes shifted away. "You read the rap sheet of ex-con Donald Hutchinson. Our last name is Hutch-*i*-son, not Hutch-*in*-son."

Alex's heart sunk. What a sucker she'd been! "So there weren't any car break-ins and stolen stereos? The police didn't set any trap tonight?"

Matthew hooted. "Boy, you're dumber than you look."

"And you're an idiot! What's the matter with you?"

"Hey, lay off. I didn't know you'd go nuts with it. I was just sick of your snotty attitude."

"*My* attitude? What do you expect, after researching me on the Internet, then telling the whole health class about my dad?"

"Oh, that." Matthew pulled on his earring. "I didn't research you anywhere. I heard your granddad tell my dad where you were born—and why you got sent up here." He swallowed, and his Adam's apple bobbed up and down. "What's the big deal anyway? No one in health knew I was talking about you."

"If you didn't do a people search, then how did you get my e-mail address to send me Onyx messages?" Alex stopped just short of snarling. "My grandpa sure didn't tell you *that.*"

"Your grandma did."

"Oh, come on!"

"Well, not on purpose. But she sends those little poems to everyone, including my dad and you. I just got your e-mail address off the long list." He bent so close to her that Alex could smell onions on his breath. "It didn't take an Einstein to know itstexas4me@hotmail.com was you."

Alex turned and watched Hutch as he zigzagged through the groups of men, shaking hands, patting backs, laughing, hugging. How could she have been so wrong about everything?

It wasn't just Onyx's messages. She'd been suspicious long before that. She hadn't liked Hutch's rumpled clothes, his clunker car, his odd hours, or how he dug through the trash. She'd assumed—without knowing any facts—that he was conning her grandparents out of their savings, when he obviously used their donations at the hospital.

"Does your dad have a *real* job, or just volunteer?" Alex asked.

"A real job. He's a counselor here. Some days, some nights, whenever the patients need him." A note of reluctant admiration crept into his voice. "He gets calls at weird hours sometimes."

Then light glimmered for Alex, and she hated what she saw. "He walks to work sometimes, doesn't he?" she asked, knowing the answer even before Matthew nodded.

"Yeah, he likes the fresh air. Why?"

"No reason." But when she'd observed him walking down the street at odd hours, Alex had decided he was a worthless bum or a felon scouting out his next break-in. And all along he'd just been a counselor at the vets' hospital, on call to help when patients needed him. And now she'd managed to get his funding cut off. Someone in the Neighborhood Watch group must have sent the hospital personnel Hutch's "criminal record."

"I like the pets idea, but why lock the cats in your basement?"

"We can't have pets. Landlady freaks out." Matthew shrugged. "Dad picks up strays, gets rid of their fleas, then brings them here. They're only at our house for a day or two, tops."

"And his visits to the pawnshop?"

"Nosy Nancy Drew! How'd you know about that? That's where he gets prizes for his shows." The sneer was back in his voice. "He does *magic* shows, can you believe it? Sometimes the pop-can money pays for prizes. Or other donations, like when youth groups do *cleaning* projects."

Alex winced at his reference to the kitchen cleanup. No matter how she looked at it now, she'd stolen that fifty dollars. Was it too late to get a refund on her bus ticket?

She had to return the money—now that she knew what it was used for—and find a way to undo the damage she'd done. Then, after she got a job somewhere and earned the money fair and square, she'd still go home to Texas. Or better yet, send her mom a bus ticket to come north.

Matthew leaned against the wall, his eyes at half-mast. "I don't know why Dad bothers working here. These inmates are all a few megs short of a gig, if you get my meaning."

Alex whirled around and jabbed Matthew in the chest.

"Your dad really cares about these guys. If you hadn't sent me that crook's Web site, things never would have gone this far."

Matthew pushed her hand away, jammed his hands in his back pockets, turned, and sauntered out the open doors.

Just then Morgan, Amber, Jamie, and Maya rushed over, followed by Coach Short, still sporting his long black cape. Alex felt a sudden rush of warmth at the sight of her friends, these "hypocrites" who were spending their Saturday night entertaining at a vets' hospital.

Coach swirled his cape up and around Alex's shoulders. "Glad you could make it, Shorty. Long time, no see."

"I meant to talk to you about that." Alex glanced from one team member to another. Now that she'd decided to stay, she felt horrible about walking off the team. Would they let her come back? Would the school rules even allow that? Alex took a deep breath. "Guys, is it too late to ask for my place back on the team?"

The silence was deafening. Jamie studied the wooden floor as if she'd never seen one before. Maya and Amber exchanged surprised glances, and Alex could read the doubt there. Morgan alone grinned.

Coach twirled an invisible mustache. "It's not that we wouldn't like to have you swimming freestyle again," he finally said. "I just wonder . . Do you understand how much you let your teammates down when you quit?"

Alex steeled herself to meet Coach's eyes. "I'm really sorry I did that." She gulped. "I can't tell you why right now, but I thought I was moving back to Texas soon."

"You changed your mind?" Morgan interrupted.

"Yeah. Some things look different tonight." Alex cleared her throat. "Anyway, I'd really like to come back. Can I?"

"Well now, that's not just up to me." Harrison Short gazed at the rest of the relay team, one by one. "What do you think, girls?"

Simultaneously, Morgan, Maya, and Jamie glanced at Amber, as if expecting her to answer for them all. Amber brushed her hair back from her face. "I guess I have a question first." Her smile was uneasy. "How committed do you feel to the team? I mean, will you be there for us from now on?"

Alex wrapped her baggy jacket tightly around her, as if hugging herself. "If you let me back on the team, I'll be there for every single practice and meet. I promise."

Coach Short removed his cape and folded it over his arm. "I'd have some requirements myself. Every afternoon next week, you'll swim extra laps to get back up to speed."

"No problem."

After a pause that lasted an eternity, Coach finally grinned. "Seems it's unanimous. Welcome back."

Morgan gave her a thumbs-up sign, and the others smiled.

Alex grinned back, glad to be on the team again. It was better this way. She still had to find out right away about her mom. That was still critical. Maybe she and her grandparents could persuade her mom to move up to Indiana with them till her dad stopped drinking. Surely they could work something out. For now, Alex had a good home and good friends, much better than she'd realized.

Amber waved her curly wig to get everyone's attention. "Time to adjourn to the Gnosh Pit. Alex, you come, too."

"I'd like to . . ." Alex took a deep breath. "But first I need to tell y'all a long story . . ."

Two hours later, Alex was back home in her spotless bedroom. She flipped on the heater, then curled up on the bed with Maverick. The last two hours had passed in a huge blur.

After Alex told her friends the whole story, Amber took Alex to the Greyhound terminal on the way to the Gnosh Pit. There Alex cashed in her bus ticket. Her face radiated heat as she handed over fifty dollars of it to Amber for the youth project.

Then she bought a round of chocolate shakes at the Gnosh Pit, bumping shoulders with her friends in the cramped booth, listening to them torment each other about boys and grades and their pitiful vaudeville performance . . .

Maverick stretched when Alex shifted to her back and stared at the cracked ceiling. She hadn't realized how much her mom's old bedroom felt like her own until she'd walked in earlier tonight. It felt *safe*, and Alex loved that. Yes, there were a zillion old-fashioned rules to follow, but her grandparents just wanted to protect her.

She wondered if her mom ever regretted running away when

she was sixteen. Even Alex had to agree with Grandpa that it hadn't solved anything. Maybe tomorrow, after church, she'd tell her grandparents the whole truth about her life in Texas. Alex loved her dad, but she was still scared for her mom. Her grandparents could invite her mom up for a visit—Alex could buy the bus ticket—and then maybe Alex could persuade her to stay.

But first, Alex thought, *there's something I have to do.*

Rolling off the bed, she sat down at the computer and logged on to her e-mail account. She opened a new message, breathed deeply for a moment, then began typing up a *true* biography of her next-door neighbor. She described Hutch's counseling, his service projects with the vets, and his work with the youth group at church. She apologized for passing along her ungrounded suspicions, then explained about the misspelled last name and the resulting mix-up and loss of funding.

When she was done, she reread it several times, correcting and adding. Finally she was satisfied that she'd done the best she could to undo the damage. At the end she asked for help in getting the truth out, signed her name, then added "Please Forward." She clicked *Send,* watched the screen flicker, then clear.

It was done.

Then she wrote her mom a long, newsy letter about Maverick, the swim team, helping Grandpa with information from the Internet, and computer geek Matthew who lived next door. By the time she finished more than an hour later, her shoulders ached.

She stretched her arms high overhead, then checked the chat

room, just in case anyone was still up. Jamie and Morgan were there, and Alex grinned when she saw their quick reactions when she "entered" the room. This was *her* chat room too. She belonged there!

rembrandt: Hey, 2-step! Glad u could join us!

jellybean: We're all so psyched ur back on the team!

TX2step: I'm jazzed 2. Thanx 4 letting me try again.

jellybean: no problem! Right, Jamie?

rembrandt: totally! Alex, i have 2 admit i enjoyed being
    served fries by u tonite @the gnosh!

TX2step: That's ok. U work hard. I admire how nice u r
    2 the dorky customers.

jellybean: Speak 4 yourself!

TX2step: I didn't mean us! We R kewl!

Alex grinned at her last line. *Us. We.* Those were great words. And tonight, for the first time, they seemed to fit her. Just then her stomach growled. How could she be hungry again already?

TX2step: Got 2 feed my face, then catch some zzzz's.
    Grandpa rings the church bell early here. CUL8R.

Padding downstairs, Alex heard her grandparents come in the back door. "You were out late," she said as she entered the kitchen. "How was the potluck?"

"Wonderfully fattening." Her grandmother patted her stomach. "We had a fascinating slide show afterward about mission trips to the former Soviet Union."

Alex grinned to herself. Whatever tripped their trigger. "I'm starving. Any leftovers?"

"Three meatballs and a brownie," Grandma answered. "Let me warm them up for you."

As the meatballs reheated in the microwave, Alex soaked up the peace in the kitchen like a dry sponge in water. Yes, this was just what her mom needed, she decided. She'd definitely ask her grandparents about it tomorrow.

"Don't forget this," her grandfather said, handing Grandma a huge yellow B-12 megavitamin.

"Yes, Doctor."

Alex grinned, then retrieved the meatballs when the microwave beeped. She practically inhaled them, then took the brownie back upstairs with her. She reached to shut the computer down when she noticed the green arrow. She had mail! She clicked on the message:

Subject: re: apology
From: Onyx <onyx321@aol.com>
Reply to all: <neighborhood.listserv>

Addition to Alex's message. I tricked her into thinking my dad had a felony rap sheet to get back at her for

being so judgmental of us. But I went too far. My dad
has no police record. Please put in a good word for him
at the VA hospital. Matthew

Well, well, well. What do you know? Alex brushed her hair
back off her face. She hadn't intended to tell the Neighborhood
Watch group about Matthew, although she planned to tell her
grandparents the whole story in the morning before church. She
didn't want them to hear about it from Hutch first.

Alex slowly reread Matthew's message. Talk about a change
of heart. She wasn't sure she could handle any more shocks
today. What was it Grandpa had said about loving thy neighbor
instead of judging them? She thought of Hutch and Matthew,
two neighbors she'd done nothing but judge since meeting
them. But *love* them instead? Not hardly!

Still, Matthew was smart. He loved computers, and he didn't
dress preppy and act cool like that senior snob, Ryan Thomas.
Maybe, just *maybe*, he wouldn't be so bad to know after all.
Some day. *Maybe.*

Who could tell? After all, Alex thought with a shiver, it was
the frozen tundra of Indiana. Anything was possible.

Net Ready, Set, Go!

I hope my words and thoughts please you.
Psalm 19:14

The characters of TodaysGirls.com chat online in the safest—and maybe most fun—of all chat rooms! They've created their own private Web site and room! Many Christian teen sites allow you to create your own private chat rooms, and there are other safe options.

Work with your parents to develop a list of safe, appropriate chat rooms. Earn Internet freedom by showing them you can make the right choices. *Honor your father and your mother. . . Deuteronomy 5:16*

Before entering a chat room, you'll select a user name. Although you can use your real name, a nickname is safer. Most people choose one that says something about who they are, like Amber's name, faithful1. Don't be discouraged if the name you select is already taken. You can use a similar one by adding a number at its end.

No one will notice your grammar in a chat room. Don't worry if you spell something wrong or forget to capitalize. Some people even misspell words on purpose. You might see a sentence like How R U?

But sometimes it's important to be accurate. Web site and e-mail addresses must be exact. Pay close attention to whether letters are upper or lowercase. Remember that Web site addresses don't use some punctuation marks, such as hyphens and apostrophes. (That's why the "Today's" in TodaysGirls.com has no apostrophe!) And instead of spaces between words, underlines are used to_make_a_space. And sometimes words just run together like onebigword.

When you're in a chat room, remember real people are typing the words that appear on your screen. Treat them with the same respect you expect from them. Don't say anything you wouldn't want repeated in Sunday school. *Do for other people what you want them to do for you (Luke 6:31).*

Sometimes people say mean, hurtful things—things that make us angry. This can happen in chat rooms, too. In some chat rooms, you can highlight a rude person's name and click a button that says, "ignore," which will make his or her comments disappear from your screen. You always have the option to switch rooms or sign off. If a particular person becomes a continual problem, or if someone says something especially vicious, you should report this problem user to the chat service. *Ask God to bless those who say bad things to you. Pray for those who are cruel (Luke 6:28-29).*

Remember that Internet information is not always factual. Whether you're chatting or surfing Web sites, be skeptical about information and people. Not everything on the Internet is true. You don't have to be afraid of the Internet, but you should always be cautious. Practice caution with others even in Christian chat rooms.

It's okay to chat about your likes and dislikes, but *never* give out personal information. Do not tell anyone your name, phone number, address, or even the name of your school, team, church, or neighborhood. Be cautious. . . . *You will be like sheep among wolves. So be as smart as snakes. But also be like doves and do nothing wrong. Be careful of people (Matthew 10:16-17).*

STRANGER ONLINE

16/junior
e-name: faithful1
best friend: Maya
site area: Thought for the Day

Confident. Caring. Swimmer. Single-handedly built
TodaysGirls.com Web site. Loves her folks.
Big brother Ryan drives her nuts! Great friend.
Got a problem? Go to Amber.

AMBER
THOMAS

JAMIE CHANDLER

PORTRAIT OF LIES

15/sophmore
e-name: rembrandt
best friend: Bren
site area: Artist's Corner

Quiet. Talented artist. Works at the Gnosh Pit
after school. Dad left when she was little.
Helps her mom with younger sisters Jordan and
Jessica. Babysits for Coach Short's kids.

ALEX DIAZ

TANGLED WEB

14/freshman
e-name: TX2step
best friend: Morgan
site area: to be determined . . .

Spicy. Hot-tempered Texan. Lives with grandparents because
of parents' problems. Won state in freestyle swimming at her
old school. Snoops. Into everything. Break the rules.

R U 4 REAL?

16/junior
e-name: nycbutterfly
best friend: Amber
site area: What's Hot—What's Not
(under construction)

MAYA CROSS

Fashion freak. Health nut. Grew up in New York City. Small town drives her crazy. Loves to dance. Dad owns the Gnosh Pit. Little sis Morgan is also a TodaysGirl.

BREN MICKLER

LUV@FIRST SITE

15/sophmore
e-name: chicChick
best friend: Jamie
site area: Smashin' Fashion: (under construction)

Funny. Popular. Outgoing. Spaz. Cheerleader. Always late. Only child. Wealthy family. Bren is chatting—about anything, online and off, except when she's eating junk food.

CHAT FREAK

14/freshman
e-name: jellybean
best friend: Alex
site area: Feeling All Write

MORGAN
CROSS

The Web-ster. Spends too much time online. Overalls. M&Ms. Swim team. Tries to save the world. Close to her family—when her big sister isn't bossing her around.

Cyber Glossary

Bounced mail An e-mail that has been returned to its sender.

Chat A live conversation—typed or spoken through microphones—among individuals in a chat room.

Chat room A "place" on the Internet where individuals meet to "talk" with one another.

Crack To break a security code.

Download To receive information from a more powerful computer.

E-mail Electronic mail which is sent through the Internet.

E-mail address An Internet address where e-mail is received.

File Any document or image stored on a computer.

Floppy Disk A small, thin plastic object which stores information to be accessed by a computer.

Hacker Someone who tries to gain unauthorized access to another computer or network of computers.

Header Text at the beginning of an e-mail which identifies the sender, subject matter, and the time at which it was sent.

Homepage A Web site's first page.

Internet A worldwide electronic network that connects computers to each other.

Link Highlighted text or a graphic element which may be clicked with the mouse in order to "surf" to another Web site or page.

Log on/Log in To connect to a computer network.

Modem A device which enables computers to exchange information.

The Net The Internet.

Newbie A person who is learning or participating in something new.

Online To have Internet access. Can also mean to use the Internet.

Surf To move from page to page through links on the Web.

The Web The World Wide Web or WWW.

Upload To send information to a more powerful computer.